James Hadley Chase and The Murder Room

>>> This title is part of The Murder Room, our series dedicated to making available out-of-print or hard-to-find titles by classic crime writers.

Crime fiction has always held up a mirror to society. The Victorians were fascinated by sensational murder and the emerging science of detection; now we are obsessed with the forensic detail of violent death. And no other genre has so captivated and enthralled readers.

Vast troves of classic crime writing have for a long time been unavailable to all but the most dedicated frequenters of second-hand bookshops. The advent of digital publishing means that we are now able to bring you the backlists of a huge range of titles by classic and contemporary crime writers, some of which have been out of print for decades.

From the genteel amateur private eyes of the Golden Age and the femmes fatales of pulp fiction, to the morally ambiguous hard-boiled detectives of mid twentieth-century America and their descendants who walk our twenty-first century streets, The Murder Room has it all. **>>>**

The Murder Room
Where Criminal Minds Meet

themurderroom.com

T0352201

James Hadley Chase (1906–1985)

Born René Brabazon Raymond in London, the son of a British colonel in the Indian Army, James Hadley Chase was educated at King's School in Rochester, Kent, and left home at the age of 18. He initially worked in book sales until, inspired by the rise of gangster culture during the Depression and by reading James M. Cain's *The Postman Always Rings Twice*, he wrote his first novel, *No Orchids for Miss Blandish*. Despite the American setting of many of his novels, Chase (like Peter Cheyney, another hugely successful British noir writer) never lived there, writing with the aid of maps and a slang dictionary. He had phenomenal success with the novel, which continued unabated throughout his entire career, spanning 45 years and nearly 90 novels. His work was published in dozens of languages and more than thirty titles were adapted for film. He served in the RAF during World War II, where he also edited the RAF Journal. In 1956 he moved to France with his wife and son; they later moved to Switzerland, where Chase lived until his death in 1985.

No Orchids for Miss Blandish
Eve
More Deadly Than the Male
Mission to Venice
Mission to Siena
Not Safe to Be Free
Shock Treatment
Come Easy – Go Easy

You Must Be Kidding
A Can of Worms
Try This One for Size
You Can Say That Again
Hand Me a Fig Leaf
Have a Nice Night
We'll Share a Double Funeral
Not My Thing
Hit Them Where It Hurts

What's Better Than Money?

James Hadley Chase

An Orion book

Copyright © Hervey Raymond 1960

The right of James Hadley Chase to be identified as the author of this
work has been asserted in accordance with the Copyright, Designs and
Patents Act 1988.

This edition published by
The Orion Publishing Group Ltd
Orion House
5 Upper St Martin's Lane
London WC2H 9EA

An Hachette UK company
A CIP catalogue record for this book is available from the British Library

ISBN 978 1 4719 0343 4

www.orionbooks.co.uk

PART ONE

CHAPTER ONE

I

I HAD been playing the piano in Rusty's bar for four months or so when I met Rima Marshall.

She came into the bar one wild night with the rain pounding down on the tin roof and thunder rumbling in the distance.

There were only two customers at the bar, both drunks. There was Rusty behind the bar, aimlessly polishing glasses. Across the way in a booth, Sam the negro waiter, was reading a racing sheet. There was me at the piano.

I was playing a nocturne by Chopin. My back was turned to the entrance. I didn't see or hear her come in.

Later, Rusty told me she had come in out of the drowning rain around twenty minutes to nine. She was soaking wet, and she sat down in one of the booths to my right and behind me.

Rusty didn't like having lone women in his bar. Usually he chased them out, but as the bar was practically empty and it was raining fit to drown a duck, he let her be.

She ordered a coke, and then lighting a cigarette, she rested her elbows on the table and stared broodingly at the two drunks at the bar.

After she had been sitting there for maybe ten minutes, things began to happen.

All of a sudden the bar door crashed open and a man came in. He took four plunging steps into the bar, the way a man walks on a rolling ship, and then came to an abrupt standstill.

It was then Rima began to scream, and it was then I became aware of her and the man who had entered.

Her scream made me jerk around to stare at her.

I'll always remember my first sight of her. She was around eighteen years of age. Her hair was the colour of polished silver and her wide, large eyes were cobalt blue. She had on a scarlet light-

1

weight sweater that set off her breasts and a pair of black tight-fitting slacks. There was a grubby unkempt look about her as if she had been living rough. On a chair by her side lay a plastic mac that had a rip in the sleeve and looked on its last legs.

In repose she would have been pretty the way so many girls her age are pretty who clutter up the sidewalks of Hollywood, hunting for film work, but she wasn't in repose right at that moment.

The terror on her face was ugly to see. Her wide open mouth as it formed her continuous scream was an ugly hole in her face. She was pressing her body against the wall -like an animal trying to get back into its burrow and from her finger nails came a nerve jarring sound of scratching as she clawed at the panelling in a futile, panic-stricken quest for escape.

The man who had come in looked like something straight out of a nightmare. He was around twenty-four, small, fine-boned with a thin, pointed face that was as white as cold mutton fat. His black hair was long and plastered to his head by the rain. It hung down either side of his face in limp strands. It was his eyes that gave him his nightmare appearance. The pupils were enormous, nearly filling the entire iris, and for a moment I got the impression that he was blind. But he wasn't blind. He was looking at the screaming girl, and there was an expression on his face that had me scared.

He had on a shabby blue suit, a dirty shirt and a black tie that looked like a shoe string. His clothes were soaking wet, and from the cuffs of his trousers water dripped, forming two little puddles on the floor.

For about three or four seconds, he stood motionless, looking at Rima, then out of his thin, vicious mouth came a steady hissing sound.

Rusty, the two drunks and I stared at him. His right hand groped into his hip pocket. He pulled a wicked looking flick-knife. It had a long pointed blade that glittered in the light. Holding the knife, its blade pointing at the screaming girl, he began to move forward, the way a spider moves, quickly, slightly crabwise and the hissing grew in sound.

"Hey, you!" Rusty bawled. "Drop it!"

But he was careful to stay right where he was behind the bar. The two drunks didn't move. They sat on the bar stools and watched, their mouths hanging open.

Sam, his face suddenly grey with fear, slid under the table and out of sight.

That left me.

A hay head with a knife is about the most dangerous thing anyone can tackle, but I couldn't sit there and watch him stab the girl, and I knew that was what he was going to do.

I kicked my chair away and started for him.

Rima had stopped screaming. She pushed the table sideways so it blocked the entrance to the booth. She held onto the table, staring with blind terror at the man as he came at her.

All this took less than five seconds.

I reached him as he reached the booth.

He seemed completely unaware of me. His concentration on the girl was terrifying.

The knife flashed as I hit him

It was a wild panicky punch, but there was plenty of weight behind it. It landed on the side of his head and sent him reeling, but it was a fraction late.

The knife slashed her arm. I saw the sleeve of her sweater turn dark, and she slumped back against the wall, then slid down out of sight behind the table.

This I saw out of the corner of my eye. I was watching him all the time. He staggered back until he had got his balance then he came forward again, not looking at me, his owl-like eyes on the booth.

As he reached the table set myself and really belted him. My fist connected with the side of his jaw. The impact lifted him clean off his feet and sent him sprawling on the floor.

He lay on his back, stunned, but he still held onto the bloodstained knife. I jumped forward and stamped on his wrist. I had to stamp twice before he released his grip. I grabbed the knife and threw it across the room.

Hissing like a snake, he bounced to his feet and came at me in a horrible, purposeful rush. He was all over me before I could punch him away. His finger nails raked my face and his teeth snapped at my throat.

Somehow I flung him off, then as he came at me again, I hung one on the point of his chin that sent a jarring pain up my arm and practically tore his head off his shoulders.

He went skittling across the bar, his arms flung wide, to land up against the wall, upsetting a table and smashing a number of glasses.

He lay there, his chin pointing towards the ceiling, his breathing rasping and quick.

As I pulled the table out of the booth, I heard Rusty yelling into the telephone for the police.

Rima was bleeding. She sat huddled up on the floor, blood making a pool by her side, her face chalk-white, her big eyes staring at me.

I must have looked a pretty sight. The hay head's finger nails had ripped four furrows down the side of my face and I was bleeding nearly as badly as she was.

3

"Are you badly hurt?" I asked, squatting at her side.

She shook her head.

"I'm all right."

Her voice was surprisingly steady, and there was no longer that ugly look of terror on her face. She was looking past me at the hay head as he lay unconscious against the wall. She looked at him the way you would look at a hairy-legged spider that suddenly appears at the foot of your bed.

"Don't worry about him," I said. "He'll be quiet for hours. Can you stand?"

"You are bleeding

"And don't worry about me......

I offered her my hand. Her's was cold as she put it into mine. I got her to her feet and she leaned against me.

Then the bar door kicked open and a couple of patrolmen stormed.They looked at me, bleeding onto the floor and Rima leaning against me, her sweater sleeve blood soaked, and one of them pulled his club and started across towards me.

"Hey! He's the guy you want." I said.

The cop looked as if he were going to take a swing at my head. He paused, then looked over his shoulder at the hay head on the floor, then back at me.

"Okay, okay," the other patrolman said. "Don't rush it, Tom Let's get it all straightened out, shall we?"

Rima gave a sudden sighing moan and fainted. I just had time to take her weight before she slid to the floor.

I knelt by her, supporting her head. I felt pretty bad myself.

"Can't you do something?" I bawled at the patrolman. "She's bleeding!"

The calm cop came over. He took out a pocket knife and cut away her sleeve. He inspected the long, deep cut on her arm. He produced a first-aid pack and in less than a minute, he had strapped her arm, stopping the bleeding.

By then Rusty had explained to the other cop what it was all about, and the cop went over to the hay head and stirred him with his foot.

"Watch it! " I said, still supporting Rima. "He's a muggle smoker and he's hopped to the eyeballs."

The cop sneered at me.

"Yeah? Think I don't know how to handle a junky?"

The hay head came alive. He shot to his feet, snatched up a carafe of water from the bar and before the cop could dodge, he slammed it down on his head. The carafe burst like a bomb and the impact drove the cop onto his knees.

The hay head turned. His owl-like eyes found Rima who was just

4

coming out of her faint. Holding the broken neck of the carafe like a spear, he charged at her and he really had me scared.

I was holding her and kneeling, and in that position I was helpless. If it hadn't been for the calm cop, both she and I would have been butchered.

He let the hay head go past him, then he slammed his club down on the back of his head.

The hay head shot forward on his face, rolled away from us and the jagged neck of the bottle fell out of his hand.

The cop bent over him and snapped on the handcuffs. The other cop, cursing, leaned weakly against the bar, holding his head between his hands.

The calm cop told Rusty to call the Station House for an ambulance.

I helped Rima to her feet and sat her on a chair well away from where the hay head lay. She was shivering, and I could see the shock was hitting her. I stood by her, holding her against me while with my free hand I kept a handkerchief to my face.

In about five minutes the ambulance and a police car arrived. A couple of guys in white coats bustled in. They strapped the hay head to a stretcher and took him out, then one of them came back and fixed my face.

While this was going on, a big, red-faced plain-clothes man who had come with the ambulance and who had introduced himself as Sergeant Hammond talked to Rusty. Then he came over to Rima.

She sat limply, nursing her arm and staring at the floor.

"Let's have it, sister," Hammond said. "What's your name?

I listened because I was curious about her.

She said her name was Rima Marshall.

"Address?"

"Simmonds Hotel," naming a fifth rate joint along the waterfront. "Occupation?"

She glanced up at him, then away. There was a sullen expression on her face as she said, "I'm an extra at the Pacific Studios."

"Who is the junky?"

"He calls himself Wilbur. I don't know his other name:"

"Why did he try to cut you?"

She hesitated for a split second.

"We lived together once. I walked out on him."

"Why?"

She stared at him.

"You saw him, didn't you? Wouldn't you walk out on him?"

"Maybe." Hammond scowled, pushing his hat to the back of his head. "Well, okay. You'll be wanted in court tomorrow."

She got unsteadily to her feet.

5

"Is that all?"

"Yeah." Hammond turned to one of the cops standing by the door. "Drive her to her hotel, Jack."

Rima said, "You'd better check with the New York police. They want him."

Hammond's eyes narrowed as he stared at her.

"What for?"

"I don't know but they want him."

"How do you know?"

"He told me."

Hammond hesitated, then shrugged. He waved to the cop.

"Take her to her hotel."

Rima walked out into the rain, the cop following her. I watched her go. I was a little surprised she didn't even look at me. I had saved her life, hadn't I?

Hammond waved me to a chair.

"Sit down," he said. "what's your name?"

"Jeff Gordon."

It wasn't my real name, but a name I had been using while out in Hollywood.

"Address?"

I told him. I had a room in a rooming-house at the back of Rusty's bar.

"Let's have your version of the shindig."

I gave it to him.

"Do you think he meant business?"

"If you mean was he going to kill her, I think he was."

He blew out his cheeks.

"Well, okay. We'll want you in court tomorrow at eleven sharp." He stared at me. "You'd better take care of that face of yours. Have you ever seen her in here before?"

"No."

"It beats me how a good looking girl like her could think of living with a rat like him." He grimaced. "Girls ... thank God, I've got a boy."

He jerked his head at the remaining cop, and together they went out into the rain.

II

All this I'm telling you about took place a year after Hitler's war. Pearl Harbour seems a long way in the past now, but at that time I was twenty-one and at college, working hard to qualify as a Consulting Engineer. I was in grabbing distance of my degree when the pace of war hotted up and I couldn't resist the call to arms. My father nearly hit the ceiling when I told him I was going to volunteer. He tried to persuade me to get my degree before joining up but the thought of another six months in college while there was fighting to be done was something I couldn't face up to.

Four months later at the age of twenty-two I was one of the first to land on the beaches of Okinawa. I got an inch of red hot shrapnel in my face as I started towards the swaying palm trees that hid the Japanese guns, and that was the end of the war so far as I was concerned.

For the next six months I lay in a hospital bed while the plastic experts remodelled my face.

They made a reasonably good job of it except they left me with a slight droop in my right eyelid and a scar like a silver thread along the right side of my jaw. They told me they could fix that if I cared to stay with them for another three months, but I had had enough. The horrors I had seen in that hospital ward remain with me even now. I couldn't get out fast enough.

I went home.

My father was a manager of a bank. He hadn't much money, but he was more than ready to finance me until I had completed my studies as a consulting engineer.

To please him I went back to college, but those months in the battle unit and the months in hospital had done something to me. I found I hadn't any more interest in Engineering. I just couldn't concentrate. After a week's work, I quit. I told my father how it was. He listened, and he was sympathetic.

"So what will you do?"

I said I didn't know, but I did know I couldn't settle to book work anyway for some time.

His eyes moved from my drooping right eyelid to the scar on my jaw and then he smiled at me.

"All right, Jeff. You're still young. Why don't you go off somewhere and take a look around? I can spare you two hundred dollars. Take a vacation, then come back and settle to work."

I took the money. I wasn't proud of taking it because I knew he couldn't spare it, but right then I was in such a rotten mental state I felt I had to get away or I would crack up.

I arrived in Los Angeles with the vague idea that I might get a job on the movies. That came unstuck pretty fast.

I didn't care. I didn't want to work anyway. I hung around the waterfront for a month doing nothing and drinking too much. At that time there were a lot of guys in reserved occupations with uneasy consciences because they hadn't done any fighting, who were ready to buy drinks for guys in return for battle stories, but this didn't last

7

long. Pretty soon my money began to run out and I began to wonder what I was going to do for the next meal.

I had got into the habit of going every night to Rusty Mac-Gowan's bar. It was a bar with a certain amount of character and it faced the bay where the gambling ships are moored. Rusty had got the place up to look like a ship's cabin with port holes for windows and a lot of brasswork that drove Sam, the negro waiter, crazy to keep polished.

Rusty had been a top sergeant and he had fought the Japs. He knew what I had been up against, and he took an interest in me. He was a very good guy. He was tough and as hard as teak, but there was nothing he wouldn't have done for me. When he heard I was out of a job, he said he was planning to buy a piano if he could find someone to play it, then he grinned at me.

He had come to the right man. The only thing I could do reasonably well was to play the piano. I told him to go ahead and buy the piano and he bought it.

I played the piano in his bar from eight o'clock in the evening to midnight for thirty bucks a week. It suited me all right. The money paid for my room, my cigarettes and my food. Rusty kept me in liquor.

Every so often he would ask me how much longer I was going to stay with him. He said with my education I should be doing something a lot better than thumping a piano night after night. I told him if it suited me, it was none of his business what I did. Every so often he would ask me again, and I would give him the same answer.

Well, that was the setup when Rima walked in out of the storm. That's the background. I was twenty-three and no good to anyone. When she walked in, trouble for me walked in with her. I didn't know it then, but I found out fast enough.

A little after ten o'clock the following morning, Mrs. Millard who ran the rooming-house where I lived, yelled up the stairs that I was wanted on the telephone.

I was trying to shave around the claw marks on my face which had puffed up in the night and now looked terrible. I cursed under my breath as I wiped off the soap.

I went down the three flights of stairs to the booth in the hall and picked up the receiver.

It was Sergeant Hammond.

"We won't be wanting you in court, Gordon", he said. "We're not going ahead with the assault rap against Wilbur."

I was surprised.

"You're not?"

8

"No. That silver wig is certainly the kiss of death. She's fingered him into a twenty year rap."

"What was that?"

"A fact. We contacted the New York police. They welcomed the news that we had him like a mother finding her long lost child. They have enough on him to put him away for twenty years."

I whistled.

"That's quite a stretch."

"Isn't it?" He paused. I could hear his heavy slow breathing over the line. "She wanted your address."

"She did? Well, it's no secret. Did you give it to her?"

"No, in spite of the fact she said she just wanted to thank you for saving her life. Take my tip, Gordon, keep out of her way. I have an idea she would be poison to any man."

That annoyed me. I didn't take any advice easily.

"I'll judge that," I said.

"I expect you will. So long," and he hung up.

That evening, around nine o'clock, Rima came into the bar. She was wearing a black sweater and a grey skirt. The black sweater set off her silver hair pretty well.

The bar was crowded. Rusty was so busy he didn't notice her come in.

She sat at a table right by my side. I was playing an *etude* by Chopin. No one was listening. I was playing to please myself.

"Hello," I said. "How's the arm?"

"It's all right." She opened her shabby little bag and took out a pack of cigarettes. "Thanks for the rescue act last night."

"Think nothing of it. I've always been a hero." I slid my hands off the keys and turned so I faced her. "I know I look terrible, but it won't last long."

She cocked her head on one side as she stared at me.

"From the look of you, you seem to make a habit of getting your face into trouble."

"That's a fact." I turned and began to pick out the melody of It Had To *Be You.* Remarks about my face embarrassed me. "I hear Wilbur is going away for twenty years."

"Good riddance!" She wrinkled her nose, grimacing. "I hope I've lost him for good now. He stabbed two policemen in New York. He was lucky they didn't die. He's a great little stabber."

"He certainly must be."

Sam, the waiter, came up and looked enquiringly at her.

"You'd better order something," I said to her, "or you'll get thrown out."

"Is that an invitation?" she asked, lifting her eyebrows at me.

9

"No. If you can, buy your own drinks you shouldn't come in here."

She told Sam to bring her a coke.

"While we are on the subject," I said to her, "I don't reckon to have attachments. I can't afford them."

She stared at me blankly.

"Well, you're frank even if you are stingy."

"That's the idea. Frank Stingy, that's the name, baby."

I began to play *Body and Soul.*

Since I had got that lump of shrapnel in my face, I had lost interest in women the way I had lost interest in work. There had been a time when I went for the girls the way most college boys go for them, but I couldn't be bothered now. Those six months in the plastic surgery ward had drained everything out of me: I was a sexless zombie, and I liked it.

Suddenly I became aware that Rima was singing softly to my playing, and after five or six bars, I felt a creepy sensation crawl up my spine.

This was no ordinary voice. It was dead on pitch, slightly offbeat on the rhythm as it should be, and as clear as a silver bell. It was the clearness that got me after listening for so long to the husky torch singers who moan at you from the discs.

I played on and listened to her. She stopped abruptly when Sam came with the coke. When he had gone I swung around and stared at her.

"Who taught you to sing like that?"

"Sing? Why, nobody. Do you call that singing?"

"Yes, I call it singing. What are you like with the throttle wide open?"

"You mean loud?"

"That's what I mean."

She hunched her shoulders.

"I can be loud."

"Then go ahead and be loud. Body and Soul. As loud as you damn well like."

She looked startled.

"I'll be thrown out."

"You go ahead and be loud. I'll take care of it if it's any good. If it isn't, I don't care if you are thrown out."

I began to play.

I had told her to be loud, but what came out of her throat shook me. I expected it to be something, but not this volume of silver sound, with a knife edge that cut through the uproar around the bar like a razor slicing through silk.

The first three bars killed the uproar. Even the drunks stopped yammering. They turned to stare. Rusty, his eyes popping, leaned across the bar, his ham-like hands knotted into fists.

She didn't even have to stand up. Leaning back, and slightly swelling her deep chest, she let it come out of her as effortlessly as water out of a tap. The sound moved into the room and filled it. It hit everyone between the eyes: it snagged them the way a hook snags a fish. It was on pitch; it was swing; It was blues; it was magnificent!

We did a verse and a chorus, then I signalled to her to cut it. The last note came out of her and rolled up my spine and up the spines of the drunks right into their hair. It hung for a moment filling the room before she cut it off and let the glasses on the bar shelf settle down and stop rattling.

I sat motionless, my hands resting on the keys and waited.

It was as I imagined it would be. It was too much for them. No one clapped or cheered. No one looked her way. Rusty picked up a glass and began to polish it, his face embarrassed. Three or four of the regulars drifted to the door and went out. The conversation started to buzz again, although on an uneasy note. It had been too good for them; they just couldn't take it.

I looked at Rima and she wrinkled her nose at me. I got to know that expression of hers: it meant: 'So what? Do you think I care?'

"Pearls before swine," I said. "With a voice like that you can't fail to go places. You could sing yourself into a fortime. You could be a major sensation!"

"Do you think so?" She lifted her shoulders. "Tell me something: where can I find a cheap room to live in? I'm nearly out of money."

I laughed at her.

"You should worry about money. Don't you realise your voice is pure gold?"

"One thing at the time," she said. "I've got to economise."

"Come to my place," I said. "There's nothing cheaper, and nothing more horrible. 25 Lexon Avenue: first turning on the right as you leave here."

She stubbed out her cigarette and stood up.

"Thanks. I'll go and fix it."

She walked out of the bar, her hips swaying slightly, her silver head held high.

All the lushes up the bar stared after her. One of them was stupid enough to whistle after her.

It wasn't until Sam nudged me that I realised she had gone without paying for the coke.

I paid for it.

I felt it was the least I could do after listening to that wonderful voice.

11

CHAPTER TWO
I

I GOT back to my room just after midnight. As I unlocked my door, the door opposite opened and Rima looked at me.

"Hello," she said. "You see: I've moved in."

"I warned you it wasn't much," I said, opening my door and turning on the light, "but at least it's cheap."

"Did you really mean that about my singing?"

I went into my room, leaving the door wide open and I sat on the bed.

"I meant it. You could make money with that voice."

"There are thousands of singers out here starving to death." She crossed the passage and leaned against my door post. "I hadn't thought of competing. I think it would be easier to make money as a movie extra."

I hadn't been able to work up any enthusiasm about anything since I had come out of the Army, but I was enthusiastic about her voice.

I had already talked to Rusty about her. I had suggested she should sing in the joint, but he wouldn't hear of it. He had agreed she could sing, but he was emphatic that he wasn't having any woman singing in his bar. He said it was certain to lead to trouble sooner or later. He had enough trouble now running the bar without looking for more.

"There's a guy I know," I said to Rima, "who might do something for you. I'll talk to him tomorrow. He runs a night club on 10th Street. It's not much, but it could be a start."

"Well, thanks . . ."

Her voice sounded so flat I looked sharply at her. "Don't you want to sing professionally?" -"I'd do anything to make some money."

"Well, I'll talk to him."

I kicked off my shoes, giving her the hint to go back to her room, but she still stood there watching me with her big cobalt blue eyes.

"I'm going to hit the sack," I said. "See you tomorrow sometime. I'll talk to this guy."

"Thanks." She still stood there. "Thanks a lot." Then after a pause, she said, "I hate to ask you. Could you lend me five dollars? I'm flat broke."

I took off my coat and tossed it on a chair.

"So am I," I said. "I've been flat broke for the past six months. Don't worry your head about it. You'll get used to it."

"I haven't had anything to eat all day."

12

I began to undo my tie.

"Sorry. I'm broke too. I haven't anything to spare. Go to bed. You'll forget to be hungry when you are asleep."

She suddenly arched her chest at me. Her face was completely expressionless as she said, "I must have some money. I'll spend the night with you if you will lend me five bucks. I'll pay you back."

I hung up my coat in the closet. With my back turned to her I said, "Beat it. I told you: I don't have attachments. Get out of here, will you?"

I heard my bedroom door shut and I grimaced..Then I turned the key. After I had washed in the tin bowl on the dressing-table and changed the plaster on my face I got into bed.

I wondered about her, and this was the first time for months that I had even thought about a woman. I wondered why she hadn't got going as a singer before now. With a voice like hers, her looks and her apparent willingness, it was hard to imagine why she hadn't become a success.

I thought about her voice. Maybe this guy I knew who ran the Blue Rose night club and whose name was Willy Floyd might be interested.

There was a time when Willy had been interested in me. He had wanted me to play the piano in a three piece combination, working from eight to three o'clock in the morning. I couldn't bring myself to work with the other guys, and that was why I had thrown in with Rusty. Willy had offered me twice as much money as Rusty paid me, but the thought of having to play with the other guys choked me off.

Every now and then I got a violent itch to make more money, but the effort to get it discouraged me. I would have liked to have moved out of this room which was pretty lousy. I would have liked to have bought a second-hand car so I could go off on my own when I felt like it.

I wondered now, as I lay in the darkness, if I couldn't pick up some easy money by acting as this girl's agent. With a voice like hers, properly handled, she might eventually make big money. She might even make a fortune if she could break into the disc racket. A steady ten percent of whatever she made might give me the extra things I wanted to have.

I heard the sudden sound of sneezing coming from her room. I remembered how soaked she had been the other night when she had come into Rusty's bar. It would be her luck and mine too if she had caught cold and couldn't sing.

She was still sneezing when I fell asleep.

The next morning, a little after eleven o'clock, when I came out of my room, she was right there in her doorway, waiting for me.

13

"Hello," I said. "I heard you sneezing last night. Have you caught cold?"

"No."

In the hard light of the sun coming through the passage window, she looked terrible. Her dark ringed eyes were watery, her nose was red and her face was white and pinched looking.

"I'm going to talk to Willy Floyd right now," I said. "Maybe you'd better rest up. You look like something the cat's dragged in. Willy won't be interested if he sees you like this."

"I'm all right." She passed a limp hand across her face. "Could you spare me half a dollar for some coffee?"

"For the love of mike! Cut it out, will you? I told you: I have nothing to spare."

Her face began to sag. It wasn't a pretty sight.

"But I've had nothing to eat for two days! I don't know what I'm going to do! Can't you spare me something ... anything... ?"

"I'm broke like you!" I yelled at her, losing my temper. "I'm trying to get you a job! I can't do more than that, can I?"

"I'm starving!" She leaned weakly against the wall and began to wring her hands. "Please lend me something . . ."

"For Pete's sake! All right! I'll lend you half a buck, but you've got to pay me back"

It had suddenly occurred to me that if she was to make any kind of impression on Willy, if she was to get a job with him, and if I were going to pick up ten per cent cut, I'd have to see she didn't starve.

I went back into my room, unlocked my dressing-table drawer and found half a dollar. In this drawer I kept my week's wages I had just received from Rusty; thirty dollars. I kept my back turned so she couldn't see what was in the drawer, and I was careful to close and lock the drawer before giving her the half dollar.

She took it and I saw her hand was shaking.

"Thanks. I'll pay it back. Honest I will."

"You'd better pay it back," I said. "I've just enough to live on, and I don't reckon to finance anyone and that includes you."

I moved out of the room, shut the door and locked it and put the key in my pocket.

"I'll be right in my room if you want me," she said. "I'll just go down to the cafe across the way for a cup of coffee, then I'll be back."

"Try to brighten yourself up, will you? If Willy wants to see you tonight, he's got to see you looking a lot better than you are now. Sure you can sing?"

She nodded.

"I can sing all right."

14

"Be seeing you," I said and went down the stairs and out into the sunshine.

I found Willy in his office with a pile of twenty dollar bills in front of him. He was counting them: every now and then he would lick a dirty finger to get a better purchase.

He nodded to me, then went on counting while I propped up the wall and waited.

His office wasn't much, but neither was the night club.

Willy was always a loud dresser. His pale blue flannel suit and his hand painted tie with the phony diamond stick pin set my teeth on edge.

He put the money in his desk drawer, then leaned back and looked at me inquiringly.

"What's biting you, Jeff?" he asked. "What are you doing here?"

"I've found a girl who can sing." I said. "You'u rave about her, Willy. She's just what you've been looking for."

His round pasty face showed boredom. He was fat, short and going bald. He had a small mouth, small eyes and a small mind.

"I'm not looking for any dames who can sing. If I wanted them they are a dime a dozen, but I don't want them. When are you going to play the piano for me? It's time you got wise to yourself, Jeff. You're wasting your life."

"Don't worry about me. I'm all right where I am. You've got to hear this girl, Willy. You could get her pretty cheap and she would be a sensation. She's got looks and she's got a voice that will stand your lousy customers right on their ears."

He took a cigar from his pocket, bit off the end and spat it across the room.

"I didn't think you went for women."

"I don't. This is strictly business. I'm acting as her agent. Let me bring her around tonight. It won't cost you a dime. I want you to hear her, then we can talk business."

He shrugged his fat shoulders.

"Well, okay. I'm not promising anything, but if she's as good as you say she is I might possibly find something for her."

"She's better than I say."

He lit his cigar and blew smoke at me.

"Look, Jeff, why don't you get smart? When are you going to throw up this way of living? A guy with your education should be doing something better . . ."

"Skip it," I said impatiently. "I'm happy as I am. See you tonight," and I walked out.

I was pretty sure once Willy had heard her, he would give her a job. Maybe I could get him to pay her seventy-five a week. That would be seven and a half dollars extra in my pocket. I was also

15

pretty sure that after she had been singing at Willy's joint for a couple of weeks, people would begin to talk about her, then I could ease her into one of the plush niteries where the pay-off would mean something.

I got quite worked up about this idea. I began to imagine myself as a big-shot agent with a swank office, and in time, interviewing and fixing up the big stars.

I went straight back to my rooming-house. Now was the time to tell Rima I was going to be her agent. I wouldn't introduce her to Willy until I had her under contract. I wasn't going to be mug enough to introduce her to Willy, and then for some other guy to grab her.

I went up the three flights of stairs two at a time and walked into her room.

Carrie, the maid of all work, was stripping the bed. There was no sign of Rima.

Carrie stared at me. She was a big, fat woman who had a drunken, out-of-work husband.

She and I got along fine together. When she did my room, we talked over our troubles. She had many more than I, but she always managed to keep cheerful and she was always urging me to throw up the life I was living and go home.

"Where's Miss Marshall?" I said, pausing in the doorway.

"She checked out half an hour ago."

"Checked out? You mean she's left?"

"Why, yes. she's gone."

I felt horribly deflated.

"Didn't she leave a message for me? Didn't she say where she was going?"

"No, and she didn't leave anything for you."

"Did she pay for her room. Carrie?"

Carrie grinned, showing her big yellow teeth. The idea of anyone walking out of Mrs. Millard's establishment without paying amused her.

"She paid."

"How much?"

"Two bucks."

I drew in a long, slow breath. It looked as if I had been taken for a ride for half a dollar. She must have had money all the time. The starvation story had been an act and I had fallen for it.

I went over to my door, took out the key, put it in the lock and tried to turn it, but it wouldn't turn. I tried the handle and the door swung open. It wasn't locked. I remembered locking it before I left to see Willy, and now it was unlocked.

I had a sudden feeling of uneasiness as I went to my dressing-table drawer. That was unlocked too, and the thirty dollars that had to last me for a week had vanished.

I had been taken for a ride all right.

II

I had a pretty thin week. Rusty staked me to a couple of meals a day, but he wouldn't finance my cigarettes. Mrs. Millard let the rent ride after I had promised to pay extra the following week. I got through the next seven days somehow, and I thought a lot about Rima. I told myself if ever I ran into her, I'd give her something to remember me by. I was disappointed that I wasn't going to break into the agency racket. But after a couple of weeks, I forgot about her, and my routine, non-productive life went on as before.

Then one day, a month after she had walked out on me, taking my money, Rusty asked me if I would go into Hollywood and collect a neon sign he had ordered. He said I could borrow his car and he'd give me a couple of bucks for my trouble.

I hadn't anything better to do so I went. I collected the sign which I put in the back of the battered Oldsmobile. Then I took a drive around the film studios for something better to do.

I saw Rima outside the entrance to the Paramount Studios, arguing with the guard. I recognised her silver head as soon as saw it.

She was wearing black skin tight jeans, a red shirt and red ballet type slippers. She looked uncared for and grubby.

I slid the car into a vacant place between a Buick and a Cadillac and walked over to her.

As I approached her, the guard went into his office and slammed the door. Rima turned and started towards me, without noticing me.

She only became aware of me when she was within three or four feet of me. She came to an abrupt stop and stared at me. Recognition jumped into her eyes and a hot flush rose to her face.

She looked furtively to right and left, but there was nowhere for her to run to, so she decided to brazen it out.

"Hello," I said. "I've been looking for you."

"Hello."

I moved slightly forward so I was within grabbing distance of her if she tried to make a bolt for it.

"You owe me thirty dollars," I said and smiled at her.

"What's that supposed to be-a joke?" Her cobalt blue eyes looked everywhere but at me. "Thirty dollars for what?"

"The thirty dollars you stole from me," I said. "Come on, baby, let's have it or you and I will go to the Station House and let them sort it out."

"I didn't steal anything from you. I owe you half a dollar: no more.

My hand closed around her thin arm.

"Let's go," I said. "Don't make a scene. I'm a lot stronger than you. You're coming to the Station House and we'll get them to say who is lying and who isn't."

She made a feeble effort to break loose, but my fingers biting into her arm must have told her she didn't stand a chance for with a sudden shrug of her shoulders, she walked with me to the Oldsmobile. I pushed her in and got in beside her.

As I started the engine, she said, a sudden note of interest in her voice, "Is this yours?"

"No, baby, I've borrowed it. I'm still broke, and I'm still going to get my money out of you. How have you been getting on since the last time we met?"

She wrinkled her nose, slumping down in her seat.

"Not so good. I'm flat broke."

"Well, a little stretch in jail will help out. At least, they feed you for free in jail."

"You wouldn't send me to jail."

"That's right, I wouldn't providing you give me back my thirty dollars."

"I'm sorry." She turned, arching her chest at me and putting her hand on my arm. "I just had to have the money. I'll pay it back. I swear I will."

"Don't swear about it. Just give it to me."

"I haven't got it now. I've spent it."

"Give me your purse."

Her hand closed over the shabby little handbag.

"No!"

I swung the car to the kerb and pulled up.

"You heard what I said! Give me your purse or I'll run you to the nearest Station House."

She glared at me, her cobalt blue eyes glittering.

"Leave me alone! I haven't any money! I've spent it all."

"Look baby, I'm not interested. Give me your purse or you'll talk to the cops!"

"You'll be sorry," she said. "I mean that. I don't forget easily."

"I don't give a damn how fast you forget," I said. "Give me your purse!"

She dropped her shabby handbag into my lap.

I opened it. There were five dollars and eight cents in it, a pack - of cigarettes, a room key and a soiled handkerchief.

18

I took the money, put it in my pocket and then shutting the bag, I tossed it back to her.

As she clutched it, she said softly, "That's something I'll never forget."

"That's fine," I said. "It'll teach you not to steal from me in the future. Where are you living?"

Her face a hard mask, her tone sullen, she told me: a roominghouse not far from where we were.

"That's where we are going."

Following her sullen directions, I drove to the rooming house that was a shade dirtier and a shade more dilapidated than the one I lived in, and we got out of the car.

"You are coming to live with me, baby," I told her. "You're going to earn some money singing, and you're going to pay me back what you stole from me. From now on I'm going to be your agent, and you're paying me ten per cent of whatever you make.

We're going to get it down in writing, but first, you're going to pack and get out of this joint."

"I'll never make any money out of singing."

"You leave me to worry about that," I said. "You're going to do what I tell you or you'll go to jail. Please yourself what you do, only hurry up and make up your mind."

"Why don't you leave me alone? I tell you I won't earn anything by singing."

"Are you coming with me or are you going to jail?"

She stared at me for a long moment. The smouldering look of hate in her eyes didn't bother me. I had her where I wanted her and she could hate me as much as she liked. She was going to pay me back my money.

Shrugging, she said, "All right, I'll come with you."

It didn't take her long to pack. I had to part with four of her dollars to take care of the room, then I drove her back to my rooming-house.

The room she had had was still empty so she moved back in. While she was unpacking, I wrote out an agreement, full of legal phrases that didn't mean a thing but looked impressive and made me her agent on a ten per cent basis.

I took it into her room.

"Sign here," I said, pointing to the dotted line.

"I'm not signing anything," she said sullenly.

"Sign this or we'll take a walk to the Station House."

Again that look of smouldering hate came into her eyes, but she signed.

"Okay," I said, putting the paper in my pocket, "tonight we're going to the Blue Rose and you're going to sing. You're going to

19

sing as you've never sung before, and you'll get an engagement worth seventy five bucks a week. I take ten per cent of that and the thirty bucks you owe me. From now on, baby, you're working first for me, then for yourself."

"I'm not going to earn anything: you wait and see."

"What's the matter with you?" I stared at her. "With that voice you could make a fortune."

She lit a cigarette and drew smoke down into her lungs. She suddenly seemed listless and she slumped in the chair as if her backbone had melted.

"Okay. Anything you say."

"What are you going to wear?"

Making an obvious effort, she got up and opened the ward-robe. She had only one dress and that wasn't much, but I knew the Blue Rose didn't go in for bright lights, and I thought the dress would get by in a pinch. It would have to.

"Couldn't I have something to eat?" she asked, flopping on the chair again. "I haven't eaten all day."

"That's all you think about-eating. You'll eat after you've got the job and not before. What did you do with all that money you stole from me?"

"I lived on it." Her face was sullen again. "How else do you imagine I've lived this past month?"

"Don't you ever work?"

"When I can."

I asked her what I had been wondering about ever since I first met her.

"How did you get hooked up with that junky, Wilbur?"

"He had money. He wasn't stingy like you."

I sat on the bed.

"Where did he get it from?"

"I don't know. I didn't ask him. There was a time when he ran a Packard. If he hadn't had trouble with the cops we'd be still riding in it."

"When he ran into trouble, you walked out on him?"

She put her hand inside her shirt and adjusted her bra. strap.

"Why not? The cops were after him. It was nothing to do with me so I skipped."

"That was in New York?"

"Yes."

"How did you get the fare down here?"

Her eyes shifted.

"I had some money. What's it to you?"

"I bet you helped yourself to his money as you helped yourself to mine."

20

"Anything you say," she said indifferently. "Think what you like."

"What are you going to sing tonight? You'd better start with Body and Soul. What do you know for an encore?"

"What makes you think there will be an encore?" she said, her expression sullen again.

I controlled the urge to slap her.

"We'll keep to the old ones. Do you know *Can't Help Loving That Man?*"

"Yes".

That was the one. With that loud, silver tone she would really knock them with that.

"Fine." I looked at my watch. It was getting on for quarter past seven. "I'll be right back. You get changed. See you in about an hour."

I went over to the door and took the key.

"Just so you don't get ideas of running away, baby, I'm going to lock you in."

"I won't run away."

"I'll take care you don't."

Going out, I shut the door and locked it.

I delivered the neon sign to Rusty and told him I wouldn't be in that evening.

He stared at me and began scratching his head in an embarrassed way.

"Look, Jeff, it's time we had a little talk. Your piano playing isn't appreciated here. I can't go on paying you thirty bucks a week. Look, be sensible and go home. The life you're leading here is no good to you. Anyway, I can't keep you on. I'm getting a juke box. This is your last week."

I grinned at him.

"Okay, Rusty. I know you mean well, but I'm not going home. The next time you see me I'll be riding in a Cadillac."

I wasn't worried about losing the thirty bucks a week. I was certain Rima would be in the money in a few weeks. With that voice she couldn't miss. I was sure of it.

I called up Willy Floyd and told him I was bringing Rima for him to hear around half-past nine.

He said all right, but he didn't sound enthusiastic. Then I went back to the rooming-house, unlocked Rima's door, and looked in.

She was lying on the bed, asleep.

There was plenty of time so I let her sleep and going into my room, I shaved and put on a clean shirt. I took my tuxedo from the closet and spent a little time sponging and pressing it. It was on its last legs, but it would have to do until I got enough money to buy another.

21

At a quarter to nine I went into her room and woke her up. "Okay, champ," I said. "Get moving. You have half an hour." She seemed pretty listless, and I could see it was an effort for her to drag herself off the bed.

Maybe she really was hungry, I thought. I couldn't expect her to give a performance if she was as bad as she looked.

"I'll send Carrie out for a sandwich," I said. "It'll be up here by the time you're dressed."

"Anything you say."

Her indifference began to worry me. I left her as she began to strip off her jeans. I went down to where Carrie was airing herself on the doorstep.

I asked her to get me a chicken sandwich.

She came back with it in a paper bag about ten minutes later and I took it into Rima's room.

Rima had got her dress on and was sitting staring at herself in the fly blown mirror. I dropped the bag into her lap, but she brushed it off, grimacing.

"I don't want it."

"For the love of mike ... !"

I caught hold of her arms and hauled her to her feet and gave her a hard little shake.

"Snap out of it, will you! You're going to sing tonight! This is your big chance! Come on! Eat this goddam sandwich. You're always moaning about your hunger! Well, go ahead and eat it!"

She picked up the bag, took out the sandwich and began to nibble at it. When she got to the chicken she hurriedly put the sandwich down.

"If I eat any more, I'll throw up."

I ate the sandwich myself.

"You make me tired," I said with my mouth full. "There are times when I wish I'd never met you. Well, come on! Let's go. I told Willy we would be there at half past nine."

Still eating, I stepped back and looked at her. She looked like a fragile ghost as white as old ivory with dark smudges under her eyes, but in spite of that, she did manage to look interesting and sexy.

We went down the stairs and out onto the street.

It was a hot night, but as she brushed against me, walking down the street, I could feel she was trembling.

"What's the matter with you?" I demanded. "Are you cold? What is it?"

"Nothing."

She suddenly sneezed violently.

"Cut that out, will you?" I yelled at her. "You've got to sing tonight!"

22

"Anything you say."

I was getting fed up with her, but I kept thinking of that voice. If she began to sneeze all over Willy Floyd, she would make one hell of a hit with him.

We got on a street car and rode down to 10th Street. The car was full and she was pressed up hard against me. Every now and then I felt her thin body quiver into a shaking fit. She began to worry me.

"Are you all right?" I asked her. "You'll be able to sing, won't you?"

"I'm all right. Leave me alone!"

The Blue Rose was crammed with the usual hard-bitten bunch of near-successful, near-honest business men, the near-beautiful floosies, the bit players from the Studios and a sprinkling of gangsters out for an evening's relaxation.

The band was playing a slick line of hot swing. Waiters were chasing and sweating, and the atmosphere was thick enough to lean on.

I shoved Rima ahead of me until we reached Willy's office. I knocked, opened the door and moved her inside.

Willy was cleaning his nails, his feet on his desk. He looked up and scowled at us.

"Hi, Willy," I said. "Here we are. Meet Rima Marshall."

Willy stared at her and nodded. His small eyes went over her and he grimaced.

"When do we go on?" I asked.

He shrugged.

"I don't care. Now, if you like." He lowered his feet to the floor. "Are you sure she's good? She doesn't look all that hot to me."

With an unexpected flash of spirit, Rima said, "I didn't ask to come here. . ."

"Pipe down," I said. "I'm handling this." To Willy, I said, "Just wait. For that crack, she's going to cost you a hundred."

Willy laughed.

"Boy! She would have to be something for me to part with that kind of money. Well, come on. Let's hear what she can do."

We went out into the restaurant and stood around in the semidarkness until the band stopped playing. Then Willy went up onto the dias. He told the boys to take a rest, and then he announced Rima.

He didn't give her much of a build up. He said here was a little girl who would like to sing a couple of songs. Then he waved his hands to us, and we were set to go.

"As loud as you like," I said to Rima and I sat down at the piano.

23

Most of the people hadn't even bothered to stop talking. None of them gave her a hand.

I didn't care. I knew the moment she opened her mouth and let out that stream of silver sound she would stun them fast enough into silence.

Willy stood near me, frowning. He kept looking at Rima. He seemed worried about something.

Rima stood by the piano, staring expressionlessly into the smoke laden darkness. She seemed completely at ease.

I began to play.   .

She came in dead on pitch. She sang the first six or seven bars like a professional. The tone was there. The sound was pure silver. The rhythm was right.

I was watching her. Then it began to go sour. I saw her face begin to sag. She lost pitch. The tone turned brassy. Then abruptly she stopped singing and she began to sneeze. She leaned forward, sneezing, her hands hiding her face, her body shaking.

There was a horrible silence except for her sneezing. Then a buzz of voices.

I stopped playing, feeling cold chills chasing up and down my spine.

I heard Willy yelling at me: "Get that junky out of here! What the hell do you mean bringing a hop head into my place! Get her out! You hear me? Get this damned junky out of here!"

CHAPTER THREE

I

RIMA lay on her bed, her face half hidden by the pillow, her body shaking, and every now and then she sneezed.

I stood at the foot of the bed and watched her.

I should have known, I told myself. I should have recognised the symptoms. It just hadn't occurred to me that she was a junky, although the writing was up on the wall that night when I had heard her sneezing by the hour.

Willy Floyd had been mad at me. Before he had thrown us out, he had told me if I ever showed my face inside his club again he'd get his bouncer to fix me, and he meant it.

I had had a hell of a time getting Rima back to her room. She was in such a state I hadn't dared to take her in a street car. I had

had to half carry her, half drag her through the back alleys until I had got her to her room.

She was quietening down now.

I watched and I felt pretty sick.

I had lost my job with Rusty and I had got in bad with Willy Floyd. All I had got out of the evening was a drug addict in my hair.

I should have packed my bag and walked out on her. I wished I had, but I kept hearing that silver voice of hers, knowing that it could make a fortune, that I had her under contract and some of the fortune could be mine.

Suddenly she rolled over and stared at me.

"I warned you," she said breathlessly. "Now get out of here and leave me alone! "

"Okay, you warned me," I said, resting my arms on the bedrail and staring back at her. "But you didn't tell me what was wrong. How long have you been on the stuff?"

"Three years. I've got the habit." She sat up and taking out her handkerchief, she began to mop her eyes. She looked as romantic as a dirty bath towel.

"Three years? How old are you then?"

"Eighteen. What's it to you how old I am?"

"You started on the stuff when you were fifteen?" I said, horrified.

"Oh, shut up!"

"Did Wilbur feed you the stuff?"

"What if he did?" She blew her nose. "Do you want me to sing? Do you want me to be a big success? If you do, give me some money. When I've had a big enough shot, I'm wonderful. You haven't heard anything yet. Give me some money. That's all I want."

I sat on the edge of the bed.

"Talk sense. I haven't any money. If I had, I wouldn't give it to you. Listen, with that voice of yours, you could go places. I know it. I'm sure of it. We're going to get you a cure. Then when the habit's broken, you'll be okay and in the money."

"That's stale news. It doesn't work. Give me some money. Five dollars will do. I know a guy . . ."

"You're going to a hospital...."

She sneered at me.

"Hospital? They're full up with junkies like me, and they don't cure you anyway. I've been to hospital. Give me five dollars. I'll sing for you. I'll be terrific. Just give me five dollars."

I couldn't take any more of it. The look in her eyes sickened me. I had had all I wanted for one night.

25

I made for the door.

"Where are you going?" she demanded.

"I'm going to bed. Tomorrow, we'll talk about it. I've had enough for tonight."

I went into my room and locked the door.

I couldn't sleep. Soon after two o'clock I heard her door open and I heard her tip-toe down the passage. Right then I didn't care if she had packed and gone. I had had as much of her as I could take for one night.

Around ten o'clock the next morning, I got up, dressed, and went to her room, opened the door and looked in.

She was in bed, sleeping. I had only to look at her relaxed expression to know she had got a shot from somewhere. She looked pretty, with her silver hair spread out on the pillow: pretty, without that awful, scraped bony look. Somehow, she had found a sucker to part with his money.

I closed the door and went down and out into the sunshine. I walked over to Rusty's bar.

Rusty looked surprised when he saw me come in.

"I want to talk to you," I said. "This is serious, Rusty."

"Okay: talk away. What is it?"

"This girl can sing. She has a fortune in her voice. I have her under contract. This could be my big chance, Rusty. She really could make a fortune."

Rusty studied me, puzzled.

"Okay. Where's the catch? If she could, why hasn't she?"

"She's a junky."

Rusty's face wrinkled in disgust.

"So?"

"I've got to get her cured. Who do I go to? What do I do?"

"You're asking me what to do? I'll tell you." He poked my chest with a finger the size of a banana. "You get rid of her, and you get rid of her fast. You can't do a thing with a junky, Jeff. I know: I'm telling you. Okay, the quacks claim they can cure them, but for how long? A month, maybe two months, maybe even three months, then the peddlers smell them out and sell them the stuff and they start all over again. Listen, son, I like you and I'm interested in you. You have brains and education. Don't mix yourself up with trash. A girl like her isn't worth bothering about. Never mind if she can sing. Get rid of her. All she'll ever bring you is grief."

I wish I had listened to him. He was right, but nobody would have convinced me at that time. I was sure she had a fortune in her voice. All I had to do was to get her cured, and the money would roll in. I was sure of it.

"Who do I take her to, Rusty? Do you know anyone who could cure her?"

Rusty ran the back of his hand under his nose: a gesture that showed his irritation.

"Cure her? No one can cure her! What's the matter with you? Are you crazy?"

I held onto my temper. This was important to me. If I could get her cured, she would be a gold mine. I knew it. I was absolutely sure of it.

"You've been around, Rusty. You get to hear things. Who's the guy who really fixes these junkies? There must be someone. The movie world is crammed with junkies. They get cured. Who's the guy who fixes them?"

Rusty rubbed the back of his neck, scowling.

"Sure, but those folk have money. A cure costs money. There is a guy, but from what I hear he costs plenty."

"Well, okay, maybe I can borrow the money. I've got to get her cured. Who is he?"

"Dr. Klinzi," Rusty said. He suddenly grinned. "You're killing me. He's way out of your class, but he's the boy. He's the one who cured Mona Gissing and Frankie Ledder," naming two of Pacific Studio's biggest stars. "They were muggle smokers, but he fixed them."

"Where do I find him?"

"He's in the book," Rusty said. "Look, Jeff, you're making a fool of yourself. This guy costs the earth."

"I don't care what he costs so long as he can cure her. I'll sell him a piece of her. She's going to make a fortune. I feel it in my bones. With that voice, she can't, go wrong."

"You're nuts."

"Okay, so I'm nuts."

I got Dr. Klinzi's address from the telephone book. He had a place on Beverley Glyn Boulevard.

Watching me, Rusty said, "Listen to me, Jeff. I know what I'm talking about. The worst thing anyone can do is to get tangled with a junky. You can never trust them. They are dangerous. They haven't the sense of responsibility sane people have. They are crazy in the head. You have got to face that fact. It's not like dealing with normal people. They will do anything and they don't count the cost. Get rid of this girl. She'll only bring you grief. You just can't mix yourself up with a girl like her."

"Save it," I said. "What are you worrying about? I'm not asking you for any donation."

I walked out and caught the street car back to my rooming-house.

27

Rima was sitting up in bed when I walked into her room. She had on a pair of black pyjamas. With her silver hair and her cobalt blue eyes, she really looked something.

"I'm hungry.

"I'll have those words engraved on your head stone. Never mind how hungry you are. Who gave you the money for a shot last night?"

Her eyes shifted away from mine.

"I didn't have a shot. I'm starving. Will you lend me... ?"

"Oh, shut up! If I can fix it, will you take a cure?"

Her expression became sullen.

"I've got beyond a cure. I know. It's no good talking about a cure."

"There's a guy who really can fix it. If I can persuade him to take you, will you go?"

"Who is he?"

"Dr. Klinzi. He fixes all the big-shot film stars. I might be able to talk him into fixing you."

"Some chance! It'd be cheaper to give me some money. I don't want much..."

I grabbed hold of her and shook her. Her breath against my face made me feel sick.

"Will you go to him if I can fix it?" I yelled at her.

She jerked away from me.

"Anything you say."

I felt I was going out of my head myself, but I kept control of myself.

"Okay, I'll talk to him. Stay right where you are. I'll tell Carrie to bring you a cup of coffee and something to eat."

I left her.

At the head of the stairs, I called down to Carrie to get a hamburger and a coffee and take it to Rima. Then I went into my room and put on my best suit. It wasn't much. It was shiny in places, but by the time I had slicked down my hair, brushed my shoes, I didn't look too much of a bum.

I went back into Rima's room.

She was sitting up in bed, sipping the coffee. She wrinkled her nose at me.

"Gee! You look sharp."

"Never mind how I look. Sing. Go on: sing anything, but sing."

She stared at me.

"Anything?"

"Yes-sing!"

She began to sing *Smoke Gets in Your Eyes*.

The melody came out of her mouth effortlessly, like a silver stream. It crawled up my spine and into the roots of my hair. It filled the room with a clear, bell-like sound. It was better than I thought it could be.

I stood there listening, and when she had gone through the chorus, I stopped her.

"Okay, okay," I said, my heart thumping. "You stay right here. I'll be back."

I went down the stairs three at a time.

II

Dr. Klinzi's residence stood in an acre and a half of ornamental gardens, surrounded by high walls, the tops of which were studded with sharp iron spikes.

I walked up the long drive. It took me three or four minutes of fast walking before I caught sight of a house that looked like a movie set for Cosimo Medici's palace in Florence.

There was a big terrace with fifty or so steps leading up to it. The top rooms had bars to the windows.

Everything about the house and the grounds was sombre and very, very quiet. Even the roses and the begonias seemed depressed.

Well away from the drive, under the shade of the elm trees, I could see several people sitting in wheel chairs. Three or four nurses, in gleaming white overalls, fluttered around them.

I climbed the steps and rang the front door bell.

After a moment or so, the door was opened by a grey man with grey hair, grey eyes, grey clothes and a grey manner.

I gave him my name.

Wordlessly, he led me over a gleaming parquet floor to a side-room where a slim, blonde nurse sat at a desk, busy with pencil and paper.

"Mr. Gordon," the grey man said.

He pushed a chair against the back of my knees so I sat down abruptly and then went away, shutting the door after him as gently as if it were made of spun glass.

The nurse laid down her pen and said in a gentle voice and with a sad smile in her eyes, "Yes, Mr. Gordon? Is there something we can do for you?"

"I hope so." I said. "I want to talk to Dr. Klinzi about a possible patient."

"It could be arranged." I was aware that her eyes were going over my suit. "Who is the patient, Mr. Gordon?"

"I'll explain all that to Dr. Klinzi."

"I'm afraid the doctor is engaged at the moment. You can have complete confidence in me. I arrange who comes here and who doesn't."

"That must be pretty nice for you," I said, "but this happens to be a special case. I want to talk to Dr. Klinzi."

"Why is it a special case, Mr. Gordon?"

I could see I wasn't making any impression on her. Her eyes had lost their sad smile: they now looked merely bored.

"I'm an agent and my client who is a singer is a very valuable property. Unless I deal directly with Dr. Klinzi, I must go elsewhere."

That seemed to arouse her interest. She hesitated briefly, then she got to her feet.

"If you will wait a moment, Mr. Gordon, I'll see..."

She crossed the room, opened the door and disappeared from sight. There was a longish pause, then she reappeared, holding open the door.

"Will you come in?"

I entered an enormous room full of modern furniture, a surgical table and desk by a window behind which sat a man in a white coat.

"Mr. Gordon?"

Somehow he made it sound as if he were very pleased to see me.

He got to his feet. He was short, not more than thirty years of age, with a lot of blond wavy hair, slate grey eyes and a bedside manner.

"That's right. Dr. Klinzi?" I said.

"Certainly." He waved a hand to a chair. "What can I do for you, Mr. Gordon?"

I sat down, waiting until the nurse had gone away.

"I have a singer with a three year morphine habit," I said. "I want her cured. What will it cost?"

The slate grey eyes ran over me none too hopefully.

"Our charge for a guaranteed cure would be five thousand dollars, Mr. Gordon. We are in the happy position here to guarantee results."

I drew in a long, slow breath.

"For that kind of money I would expect results."

He smiled sadly. They seemed to specialise in sad smiles in this place.

"It may seem expensive to you, Mr. Gordon, but we deal only with the very best people."

"How long would it take?"

"That would depend largely on the patient. Five weeks perhaps, but if it is a very stubborn case, eight weeks: not longer."

"Guaranteed?"

"Naturally."

There was no one I knew who would be crazy enough to lend me five thousand dollars, and there was no way I could think of to raise such a sum.

I turned on the soft soap faucet.

"It's slightly more than I can afford, doctor. This girl has a great singing voice. If I can get her cured, she's going to make a lot of money. Suppose you take a piece of her? Twenty per cent of whatever she makes until the five thousand is taken care of, then three thousand on top as interest."

As soon as I had uttered the words I knew it was a mistake. His face suddenly went blank, and his eyes turned remote.

"I'm afraid we don't do that kind of business here, Mr. Gordon. We are very booked up. Our terms are, and have always been, cash. Three thousand on entry, and two thousand when the patient leaves."

"This is a very special case..."

His well-cared-for finger moved to a button on his desk.

"I'm sorry. Those are our terms."

The finger pressed the button lovingly.

"If I can raise the money, the guarantee is really guaranteed?'

"You mean the cure? Of course."

He was standing now as the door opened and the nurse drifted in. They both gave me sad smiles.

"Should your client want to come to us, Mr. Gordon, please let us know soon. We have many commitments and it may be difficult, if not impossible, to fit her in."

"Thanks," I said. "I'll think it over."

He gave me his cool white hand as if he was conferring a favour on me, then I was ushered out by the nurse.

On my way back to the rooming-house, I thought about what he had said, and for the first time in my life I really felt the urge for some money. But what hope had I of laying my hands on five thousand dollars? If I could raise that sum by some miracle, if I could get Rima cured, I was absolutely certain she would go to the top and I would go with her.

As I was walking along, brooding, I passed a big store that sold gramophone and radio equipment. I paused to look at the brightly coloured sleeves of the long play discs, imagining how Rima's photograph would look on one of those sleeves.

A notice in the window caught my attention.

Record Your Voice on Tape.
A three minute recording for only $2.50
Take your voice home in your pocket and surprise
your friends.

That gave me an idea.

If I could get Rima's voice recorded, I wouldn't have the worry of wondering when I got her an audition that she would blow up as she had done at the Blue Rose. I could hawk the tape around, and maybe get someone interested enough to advance the money for her cure.

I hurried back to the rooming-house.

Rima was up and dressed when I walked into her room. She was sitting by the window, smoking. She turned and looked expectantly at me.

"Dr. Klinzi says he can cure you," I said, sitting on the bed, "but it costs. He wants five thousand bucks."

She wrinkled her nose, then shrugging, she turned back to stare out of the window.

"Nothing is impossible," I said. "I have an idea. We're going to record your voice. There's a chance someone in the business will put up the money if he hears what you can do. Come on, let's go."

"You're crazy. No one will pay out that kind of money."

"Leave me to worry about that. Let's go."

On the way to the store, I said, "We'll do *Some of these Days*. Do you know it?"

She said she knew it.

"As loud and as fast as you can."

The salesman who took us into the recording room was supercilious and bored. It was pretty obvious he looked on us as a couple of bums with nothing better to do than to squander two dollars fifty and waste his time.

"We'll have a run through first," I said, sitting down at the piano. "Loud and fast."

The salesman switched on the recorder.

"We don't reckon to have rehearsals," he said. "I'll fix it as she goes."

"We'll have a run through first," I said. "This may not be important to you, but it is to us."

I began to play, keeping the tempo a shade faster than it is usually taken. Rima came in loud and fast. I looked across at the salesman. Her clear silver notes seemed to have stunned him. He stood motionless, gaping at her.

I've never heard her sing better. It was really something to hear.

We did a verse and a chorus, then I stopped her.

"Sweet grief!" the salesman said in a hushed whisper. "I've never heard anything like it!"

Rima looked at him indifferently and said nothing.

"Now we'll record it. Okay for sound?" I said.

"Go ahead," the salesman said, adjusting the recording knob.

"Ready when you are," and he started the tape running through the recording head.

Rima, if anything, was a shade better this time. She certainly had all the professional tricks, but that didn't matter. What counted was her tone. The notes came out of her throat with the clearness of a silver bell.

When the recording was finished, the salesman offered to play it back over an electrostatic speaker.

We sat down and listened.

With the volume right up and the filters on to cut out the valve hiss, her voice sounded larger than life and terrific. It was the most exciting recording I have ever listened to.

"Phew!" the salesman said as he took off the tape, "how you can sing! You should let Al Shirely hear this recording. He would go crazy about it."

"Al Shirely? Who is he?" I asked.

"Shirely?" The salesman looked amazed. "Why, he's the boss of the Californian Recording Company. He's the guy who discovered Joy Miller. Last year she made five discs. Know what she made from them? A half a million! And let me tell you something! She doesn't know how to sing if you compare her with this kid. I'm telling you! I've been in the business for years. I've never heard anyone to touch this kid. You talk to Shirely. He'll fix her when he hears this tape."

I thanked him. When I offered him the two dollars fifty for the recording, he waved it aside.

"Forget it. It's been an experience and a pleasure. You talk to Shirely. It would give me a big bang if he took her up." He shook hands with me. "Good luck. You can't fail to go places."

I was pretty worked up as we walked back along the waterfront to the rooming-house. If Rima was a better singer than Joy Miller, and this salesman should know what he was talking about then she could earn enormous money. Suppose in her first year she did click, and made half a million! Ten per cent of half a million sounded pretty good to me.

I looked at her as we walked along, side by side. She moved listlessly, her hands deep in the pockets of her jeans.

"This afternoon I'll talk to Shirely," I said. "Maybe he'll spring the five thousand for your cure. You heard what the guy said. You could go right to the top."

"I'm hungry," she said sullenly. "Can't I have something to eat?"

"Are you listening to what I'm saying?" I stopped and pulled her around so she faced me. "You could make a fortune with that voice of yours. All you want is a cure."

"You're kidding yourself," she said, jerking free. "I've had a cure. It doesn't work. How about something to eat?"

"Dr. Klinzi could fix you. Maybe Shirely would advance the money when he hears the recording."

"Maybe I'll grow wings and fly away. No one is going to lend us that kind of money."

Around three o'clock that afternoon, I borrowed Rusty's car and drove over to Hollywood. I had the tape in my pocket and I was really worked up.

I knew it would be fatal to tell Shirely that Rima was a junky. I felt sure, if he knew, he wouldn't touch her.

Somehow I had to persuade him to part with a five thousand dollar advance. I had no idea how I was going to do it. Everything depended on how he reacted to the tape. If he was really enthusiastic, then I might get him to part with the money.

The Californian Recording Company was housed within a stones throw of the M.G.M. Studios. It was a two-storey building that covered practically an acre of ground. There was the usual reception office outside the gates with two tough-looking, uniformed guards to take care of the unwelcomed visitors.

It was when I saw the size of the place, I realised what I was up against. This was big-time, and I had an abrupt loss of confidence. I was suddenly aware of my shabby suit and my scruffy shoes.

One of the guards moved forward as I came up. He looked me over, decided I was of no importance and asked in a rough-tough voice what I wanted.

I said I wanted to talk to Mr. Shirely.

That seemed to kill him.

"So do twenty million others. You gotta appointment?"

"No."

"Then you don't see him."

This was the moment for a bluff. I was desperate enough to swear my father had been a negro.

"Well, okay. I'll tell him how efficient you are," I said. "He told me to look in when I was passing, but if you won't let me in, that's his loss, not mine."

He did a quick double-take.

"He said that?"

"Why not? He and my father were at college together.

He lost his aggressive look.

"What did you say your name was?"

"Jeff Gordon."

"Just hang on a moment."

He went into the reception office and talked on the telephone. He came out after a while, unlocked the gates and waved me in.

"Ask for Miss Weseen."

At least that was one step forward.

Dry mouthed and with my heart thumping, I walked up the drive to the imposing entrance hall where a boy in a sky blue uniform and brass buttons that glittered like diamonds, conducted me along a corridor lined on either side by polished mahogany doors to a door marked with a brass plate:

Mr. Harry Knight and Miss Henrietta Weseen.

The boy opened the door and waved me in.

I walked into a large room decorated in dove grey where about fifteen people sat around in lounging chairs looking like the legion of the lost.

I had no time to concentrate on them before I found myself staring into emerald green eyes that were as hard as glass and just as expressionless.

The owner of the eyes was a girl of about twenty four, a redhead with a Munro bust, a Bardot hip line and an expression that would have frozen an Eskimo.

"Yes?"

"Mr. Shirely, please."

She patted her hair and regarded me as if I were something out of a zoo.

"Mr. Shirely never sees anyone. Mr. Knight is engaged. All these people are waiting for him." She waved a languid hand at the lost legion. "If you will give me your name and tell me your business I'll try to fit you in at the end of the week."

I could see the lie I had told the guard wouldn't cut any ice with her. She was smart, wise and lie-proof.

If I couldn't bluff her I was fixed.

I said carelessly, "A week? Too late. If Knight can't see me right now, he's going to lose money and Mr. Shirely will be annoyed with him."

Feeble stuff, but it was the best I could do.

At least everyone in the room was listening, leaning forward and pointing like gundogs.

If they were impressed, Miss Weseen wasn't. She gave me a small, bored smile.

"Perhaps you would write in. If Mr. Knight is interested he'll let you know."

At that moment the door opened behind her and a fat man, balding, nudging forty, in a fawn coloured seersucker suit, looked around the room with a hostile air and said, "Next," the way a dentist's nurse calls to the flock.

I was right by him. Out of the corner of my eye I saw a tall youth with Elvis Presley sideboards drag himself out of an armchair, clutching a guitar, but he was much too late.

I walked forward, driving the fat man back into his office, giving him a wide, confident smile.

"Hello, there, Mr. Knight," I said. "I have something for you to listen to, and when you've heard it, you'll want Mr. Shirely to hear it too."

By then I was inside the room and had shut the door with my heel.

On his desk was a tape recorder. Moving around him, I put the tape on the machine and turned the machine on.

"This is something you'll be glad to listen to," I said, talking hard and fast. "Of course, it isn't going to sound so hot on a machine like this, but hear it on an electrostatic speaker and you'll hit the ceiling."

He stood watching me, a startled expression on his fat face.

I pushed down the start button and Rima's voice came out of the speaker and hit him.

I was watching him and I saw the muscles of his face tighten as the first notes filled the room.

He heard the tape right through, then as I pressed the re-wind button, he said, "Who is she?"

"My client," I said. "How about Mr. Shirely hearing her?"

He looked me over.

"And who are you?"

"Jeff Gordon's the name. I'm in a hurry to do a deal. It's either Mr. Shirely or R.C.A. Please yourself. I came here first because R.C.A. is just that much further away."

But he was too old a hand for that kind of bluff. He grinned and sat down behind his desk.

"Don't get so intense, Mr. Gordon," he said. "I'm not saying she isn't good. She is, but I've heard better voices. We might be interested. Bring her around towards the end of the week. We'll give her an audition."

"She's not available, and she is under contract to me."

"Well, all right, then when she is available."

"The idea was for me to get a contract from you right away," I said. "If you don,t want her, I'll try R.C.A."

"I didn't say we don't want her," Knight said. "I said we want to hear her in person."

"Sorry." I tried to sound tough and business-like, but I knew I was making a poor show of it. "The fact is she isn't well. She needs toning up. If you don't want her, say so and I'll get out of here."

The door opened on the far side of the room and a small, white haired Jewish gentleman wandered in.

36

Knight got hurriedly to his feet.

"I won't be one moment, Mr. Shirely ...

There was my cue and I didn't miss it. I pressed the play back button on the recorder and turned the volume up.

Rima's voice filled the room.

Knight made to turn the recorder off, but Shirely waved him away. He stood listening. His head cocked on one side, his dark little eyes moved from me to Knight and then to the recorder.

When the tape finished and I had stopped the machine, Shirely said, "Exceptionally good. Who is she?"

"Just an unknown," I said. "You wouldn't know her name. I want a contract for her."

"I'll give you one. Have her here tomorrow morning. She could be a valuable property," and he started for the door.

"Mr. Shirely . . ."

He paused to look over his shoulder.

"This girl isn't well," I said, trying to keep the desperation out of my voice. "I need five thousand dollars to get her fit. When she is fit, she'll sing even better than that record. I'll guarantee it. She could be the sensation of the year, but she has to be got fit. Is her voice, as it is, good enough for you to gamble on a five thousand advance?"

He stared at me, his small eyes going glassy.

"What's the matter with her?"

"Nothing a good doctor can't fix."

"Did you say five thousand?"

The sweat was running down my face as I said, "She needs special treatment."

"From Dr. Klinzi?"

There seemed no point in lying to him. He wasn't the kind of man you could lie to.

"Yes."

He shook his head.

"I'm not interested. I would be interested if she was quite fit and ready to go to work. I would give you a very good contract, but I am not interested in anyone who has to go first to Dr. Klinzi before they can sing."

He went out, closing the door behind him.

I took the tape off the recorder, put it in its box and dropped the box into my pocket.

"There it is," Knight said awkwardly. "You played it wrong. The old man has a horror of junkies. His own daughter is one."

"If I can get her cured, would he be interested?"

"No doubt about it, but he would have to be sure she was cured."

He opened the door and eased me out.

CHAPTER FOUR

I

WHEN I finally got home, Rima was out. I went into my bedroom and lay on the bed. I was completely bushed.

I hadn't felt so depressed in years. From the Californian Recording Studios, I had driven to R.C.A. There they had admired Rima's voice, but when I began to talk about a five thousand dollar advance they eased me out so fast I hadn't a chance to argue with them.

I had gone to two of the bigger agents who also showed interest, but when they heard Rima was under contract to me they brushed me off in a way that made my ears burn.

The fact that Rima had gone out depressed me further. She had known I was going to see Shirely, and yet she hadn't bothered to wait in to find out the result of the interview. She had been certain nothing would come of it. Bleak experience had already taught her that any effort of mine to get her somewhere was so much waste of time. That thought depressed me even more.

I now had to face the problem of what I was going to do.

I was out of a job and I had only enough money to last me until the end of the week. I didn't even have my fare home.

I didn't want to do it, but I finally decided I would have to go home. I knew my father would be sympathetic enough not to throw my failure in my face. I would have to get Rusty to lend me the fare and persuade my father to pay him back.

I was so frustrated and depressed I felt like banging my head against the wall.

Five thousand dollars

If I could only get Rima cured, I knew she would make a hit. In a year she could make half a million and that would be fifty thousand dollars in my pocket: a lot better than crawling home and having to tell my father I had flopped.

I lay on the bed thinking like this until it got dark. Then just when I had finally made up my mind to go down and talk Rusty into lending me the money, I heard Rima come up the stairs and go into her bedroom.

I waited.

After a while she wandered in and stood at the foot of the bed, staring down at me.

"Hello," she said.

I didn't say anything.

"How about something to eat?" she said. "Have you any money?"

38

"Don't you want to hear what Shirely said?"

She yawned, rubbing her eyes.

"Shirely?"

"Yes. The boss of the Californian Recording Company. I went to see him this afternoon about you-remember?"

She shrugged indifferently.

"I don't want to know what he said. They all say the same thing. Let's go somewhere and eat."

"He said if you took a cure, he'd make a fortune for you."

"So what? Have you any money?"

I got off the bed and went over to the mirror on the wall and combed my hair. If I hadn't done something with my hands, I would have hit her.

"No, I haven't any money, and we don't eat. Clear out! The sight of you makes me sick to my stomach.'

She sat on the edge of the bed. She put her hand inside her shirt and began to scratch her ribs.

"I've got some money," she said. "I'll treat you to dinner. I'm not stingy like you. We'll have spaghetti and veal."

I turned to stare at her.

"You have money? Where did you get it from?"

"The Pacific Studios. They 'phoned just after you left. I had three hours crowd work."

"I bet you are lying. I bet you went down some dark alley with an old man with a beard!'

She giggled.

"It was crowd work. I'll tell you something else. I know where we can get that five thousand you're worrying about." I put down the comb and faced her.

"What the he'll are you talking about?"

She studied her finger nails. Her hands were grubby and her nails black rimmed.

"The five thousand for the cure."

"What about it?"

"I know where we can get it."

I drew in a long slow breath.

"There are times when I would like to beat you," I said. "You exasperate me so much one of these days I'll slap your bottom until you scream blue murder."

She giggled again.

"I know where we can get it," she repeated.

"That's wonderful. Where can we get it?"

"Larry Lowenstien told me."

I thrust my hands deep into my trousers pockets.

"Don't act cute, you dope! Who's Larry Lowenstien?"

"A friend of mine." She leaned back on her elbows, arching her chest at me. She looked as seductive as a plate of lukewarm soup. "He works for the casting director. He told me they keep more than ten thousand dollars in the casting office. They have to have it in cash to pay the extras. The lock on the door is nothing." I lit a cigarette: my hands began to shake.

"What's it to me how much money they keep in the casting office?"

"I thought we could get in there and help ourselves."

"That's quite a bright idea coming from you. What makes you imagine they wouldn't object to us taking it? Hasn't anyone told you that taking someone's money is stealing?"

She wrinkled her nose and shrugged.

"It was just an idea. If you feel that way about it, forget it." "Thanks for the advice. That's just what I'm going to do."

"Well, all right. Anything you say, but I thought you were so keen to get that money."

"I am, but not that keen."

She got up.

"Let's go and eat."

"You go. I have something to do."

She wandered to the door.

"Oh, come on. I'm not stingy. I'll treat you. You're not too proud to be treated by me, are you?"

"I'm not proud. I've something else to do: I'm going to talk to Rusty. I'm borrowing my fare home from him. I'm quitting."

She stared at me.

"What do you want to do that for?"

"I'm out of a job," I said patiently. "I can't live on air so I'm going home."

"You can get a job at the Pacific Studios. There's a big crowd scene tomorrow. They want people."

"They do? How do I get a job like that then?"

"I'll fix it. Come with me tomorrow. They'll give you a job. Now let's go and eat: I'm starving."

I went with her because I was hungry and I couldn't be bothered to argue with her any more.

We went to a small Italian restaurant and ate spaghetti which was very good and thin slices of veal fried in butter.

Half way through the meal, she said. "Did Shirely really say I could sing?"

"That's what he said. He said when you had a cure and when you were a hundred per cent fit, he would give you a contract."

She pushed aside her plate and lit a cigarette.

"It would be easy to take that money. There would be nothing to it."

40

"I wouldn't do a thing like that for you nor anyone else!"

"I thought you wanted me to have a cure?"

"Oh, shut up! To hell with your cure and to hell with you!" Someone put a nickel into the juke box. Joy Miller began to sing Some of these Days. We both listened intently. She was loud and brassy and often off-pitch. The tape I had in my pocket was much, much better than this disc.

"Half a million a year," Rima said dreamily. "She isn't so hot is she?"

"No, but she's a lot hotter than you. She doesn't need a cure. Let's get out of here. I'm going to bed."

When we got back to the rooming-house, Rima came to the door of my room.

"You can sleep with me tonight if you like," she said. "I feel in the mood."

"Well, I don't," I said, and I shut the door in her face.

I lay in bed in the darkness and thought about what she had said about all that money in the casting director's office. I kept telling myself that I had to get the idea of stealing the money out of my mind. I had sunk pretty low, but I hadn't sunk that low, but the idea kept nagging at me. If I could get her cured ... I was still pecking at the idea when I fell asleep.

The next morning, soon after eight o'clock, we took the bus into Hollywood. There was a big crowd moving through the main gates of the Pacific Studios and we tagged along behind.

"There's plenty of time," Rima said. "They won't start shooting until ten. You come with me. I'll get Larry to book you."

I went along with her.

Away from the main studio block was a number of bungalow type buildings. Outside one of them stood a tall, thin man wearing corduroy trousers and a blue shirt.

I hated the sight of him as soon as I saw him. His white puffy face was badly shaven. His eyes were close set and cunning. He looked like a pimp alert for business.

He gave Rima a jeering grin.

"Hello, sugar, coming to work your stint?" he said and then he looked at me. "Who's this?"

"A friend," Rima said. "Can he be one of the crowd, Larry?"

"Why not? The more the merrier. What's his name?"

"Jeff Gordon," Rima said.

"Okay. I'll book him." To me, he went on, "Get over to Number three studio, pal. Down the alley, second on your right!" Rima said to me, "You go ahead. I want to talk to Larry." Lowenstien winked at me.

"They all want to talk to me."

41

I went off down the alley. Half way down, I looked back. Rima was going into the office with Lowenstien. He had his arm around her shoulders and he was leaning close, talking to her.

I stood in the hot sunshine and waited. After a while, Rima came out and joined me.

"I was taking a look at that lock. There's nothing to it. The lock on the drawer where the money is kept is tricky, but I could open it, given a little time."

I didn't say anything.

"We could do it tonight. We could get lost here," she went on. "I know a place where we can hide. We'd have to stay the night here and get out in the morning. It would be easy."

I hesitated for perhaps half a second. I knew if I didn't take this risk I wasn't going to get anywhere. I realised I would have to go home and admit defeat. Once I got her cured, both of us would be in the money.

Right at that moment, all I could think of was what ten per cent of half a million dollars would mean to me.

"Okay," I said. "If you're going to do it, I'll do it with you."

II

We lay side by side in the darkness, under the big stage of Studio Three. We had been lying like that for the past three hours, listening to the tramp of feet overhead, the shouting of the technicians as they prepared the new set for tomorrow's shooting, the professional cursing of the director as they didn't do what he told them to do and did what he told them not to do.

All the morning and the afternoon, we had worked in the heat of the arc lights until dusk with three hundred other extras: that regiment of the lost who hang on to Hollywood in the hope, some day, someone will notice them and turn them into stars, and we had sweated with them and hated them.

We had been part of a crowd supposed to be watching a Championship fight. We had stood and yelled when the director had signalled to us. We had sat and booed. We had leaned forward with horror on our faces. We had jeered, and finally we had lifted the roof when the pale, thin looking kid in the ring who didn't look as if he could punch his way out of a paper bag, had brought the champion down on his knees and forced him to quit.

We had done all that over and over again from eleven o'clock until seven o'clock in the evening, and it was the hardest day's work

I have ever done in my life.

Finally, the director had broken it up.

"Okay, boys and girls," he had bawled over the loudspeaker system. "I want you all here tomorrow at nine sharp. Wear what you are wearing now."

Rima put her hand on my arm.

"Keep close to me and move fast when I tell you."

We tagged along just behind the long line of sweating extras. My heart was thumping, but I wouldn't let myself think what was ahead of me.

Rima said, "Through here," and gave me a little push.

We slipped down an alley that brought us to the back entrance of Studio Three.

It was easy to get under the stage. For the first three hours we remained like mice, scared that someone might find us, but after a while, around ten o'clock, the technicians knocked off and we had the place to ourselves.

By then I was aching for a cigarette and so was Rima. We lit up. In the feeble light of the match's flame, I saw her stretched out beside me in the dust, her eyes glittering, and she wrinkled her nose at me.

"It's going to be all right. In another half hour, we can do it."

It was then I began really to get scared.

I told myself I must be out of my mind to get involved in a thing like this. If we were caught ...

To get my mind off it, I said, "What's this guy Lowenstien to you?"

She shifted. I had an idea I had touched a sore point.

"He's nothing to me."

"Don't tell me! How did you get to know a rat like him? He takes after your pal Wilbur."

"You're a fine one to talk with your scarred face! Who do you imagine you are?"

I clenched my fist and punched her hard on her thigh.

"Shut up about my face!"

"Then shut up about my friends!"

I had a sudden idea.

"Of course-you get the stuff from him! He's got peddler written all over him."

"You hurt me!"

"There are times when I could strangle you. He's the rat you get your drugs from, isn't he?"

"What if he is? I have to get it from someone, don't I?"

"I must be nuts to have anything to do with you!"

"You hate me, don't you?"

43

"Hate doesn't come into it."

"You're the first man who hasn't wanted to sleep with me," she said, her tone bitter.

"I'm not interested in women."

"You're in as much a mess as I am only you don't seem to know it".

"Oh, go to hell!" I said, furious with her. I knew she was right. I had been in a mess ever since I had come out of hospital, and what was more, I had grown to like being in a mess.

I'll tell you something now," she said softly. "I hate you. I know you are good for me: I know you could save me, but all the same I hate you. I'll never forget how you treated me when you blackmailed me about the police. Watch out, Jeff. I'll get my own back for that even if we go into business together."

"You try anything funny with me," I said, glaring in her direction in the darkness, "and I'll give you a hiding. That's what you want: a damn good hiding."

She suddenly giggled.

"Maybe I do. Wilbur used to beat me."

I moved away from her. She was so corrupt and horrible it made me sick to be close to her.

"What's the time?" she asked.

I looked at the luminous hands of my watch.

"Half past ten."

That set my heart thumping.

"Do they have guards here?"

"Guards? What for?"

She was already crawling away from me, and I went after her. A few seconds later we were standing together in the darkness, near the exit of the Studio. We paused to listen.

There wasn't a sound.

"I'll lead the way," she said. "Keep close to me."

We moved out of the Studio into the hot, dark night. There were stars, but the moon hadn't come up yet. I could just see her as she paused to look into the darkness, the way I was looking.

"Are you scared?" she asked, moving close to me. I hated the feel of her slight, hot body, but my back was against the wall of the studio and I couldn't get away from her. "I'm not. This sort of job never scares me, but I think you're scared."

"Okay, so I'm scared." I said, shoving her away. "Does that satisfy you?"

"You don't have to be. They can't do anything to you worse than you have already done to yourself. That's something I'm always telling myself."

44

"You're nuts! What kind of talk is that supposed to be?"

"Come on," she said. "Let's get the money. It'll be easy."

She moved away into the darkness and I followed her.

All day, she had been carrying a sling bag over her shoulder.

When she paused outside the casting director's bungalow, I heard her zip the bag open.

I stood close to her, listening, aware of the thudding of my heart beats, feeling my blood pounding through my veins and I was scared silly.

I heard her fiddling with the lock. She must have been very expert. In a few seconds, I heard the lock snap back.

Together we entered the dark office. We paused, waiting for our eyes to become used to the faint light from the stars we could see through the uncurtained window. After a few seconds we could see the outline of the desk across the room.

We went over to it and Rima knelt beside it.

"You keep watch," she said. "This shouldn't take long."

I was shaking with fright by now.

"I don't want to go ahead with this" I said. "Let's get out of here!"

"Don't be a quitter!" she said sharply. "I'm not giving up now."

There was a sudden gleam of light as she turned the beam of a flashlight on the lock of the drawer. Then she sat on the floor and began to hum softly under her breath.

I waited, my heart thumping, listening to the tiny scratching noise she was making as she worked on the lock.

It's tricky," she said, "but I'll fix it in a moment."

But she didn't. The minutes dragged by: the scratching noise began to get on my nerves. Now she had stopped humming and I could hear her swearing under her breath.

"What's going on?" I asked, moving away from the window to stare over the desk at her.

"It's a toughie, but I'll beat it." She sounded quite calm. "Leave me alone. Let me concentrate!"

"Let's get out of here!"

"Oh, quiet down!"

I turned back to the window, then my heart gave a sudden bound, leaving me breathless.

Outlined against the starlit darkness I could see the head and shoulders of a man who was looking through the window.

I didn't know if he could see me. It was dark in the office, but he seemed to be staring directly at me.

His shoulders looked immense, and on his head was a flat peaked cap that turned me cold.

"There's someone out there," I said, but the words didn't get beyond my dry lips.

Rima said, "I've fixed it!"

"There's someone out there!"

"I've got it open!"

"Didn't you hear me? Someone's outside!"

"Get under cover!"

I looked wildly around the dark room. Sweat, as cold as ice, was running down my face. I started across the room as the door was flung open. The light clicked on.

The impact of the hard, bright light on me was like a blow on the head.

"Make a move and I'll blast you!

A cop voice: tough, hard and full of confidence.

I looked towards the door.

He stood in the open doorway, a .45 in his brown muscular hand, pointing at me. He was all-cop: big, broad and terrifying.

"What are you doing in here?"

Slowly, I put up my shaking hands. I had a horrible feeling he was going to shoot

"I—I—I...." me.

"Keep your hands like that!"

He didn't know Rima was crouching behind the desk. My one thought now was to cover her: to get out of the office before he found her.

Somehow I managed to get some control over my shaking nerves.

"I lost my way," I said. "I was going to sleep here."

"Yeah? You'll sleep somewhere a lot safer than here. Come on. Move slowly and keep your hands up."

I moved towards him.

"Hold it!" He was staring at the desk. "Have you been trying to bust into that?"

"No ... I tell you...."

"Back up against the wall! Move!"

I backed up against the wall.

"Turn around!"

I faced the wall.

There was a long moment of complete silence.

The only sound in my ears was the thud-thud-thud of my heart beats; then there came a violent, shattering crash of gunfire.

The sound, enormous in the room made me cringe. I looked over my shoulder, thinking the guard had walked right into Rima and had killed her.

He was standing by the desk, bent double. His smart cap had fallen off, showing a bald spot at the back of his head. His gauntlet gloves were pressed to his stomach, his gun lay on the floor.

From between the fingers of his gloves, blood began to leak, then there was a second bang of gunfire. I saw the flash of the gun coming from behind the desk.

The guard gave a strangled grunt: the sound a fighter makes when his opponent has sunk in one that really cripples. Then, slowly, he tipped over and spread out on the floor.

I stood there, staring, my hands still in the air, sick enough to throw up.

Rima straightened up from behind the desk. In her hand was a smoking .38. She looked indifferently at the guard. She hadn't even lost colour.

"There's no money," she said savagely. "The drawer's empty." I scarcely heard what she was saying.

I stared at the guard, watching the trickle of blood move out of him in a thin thread across the polished parquet floor.

"Let's get out of here!"

The urgent rasp in her voice brought me to my senses.

"You've killed him!"

"He would have killed me, wouldn't he?" She stared coldly at me. "Come on, you fool! Someone will have heard the shooting!"

She started across the room, but I grabbed her arm, jerking her around.

"Where did you get that gun?"

She wrenched free.

"Oh, come on! They'll be here in a moment!"

Her indifferent, glittering eyes horrified me.

Then somewhere in the outer darkness I heard a siren start up. Its moaning note chilled me.

"Come on! Come on!"

She ran out into the darkness and I went after her.

Lights were coming on all over the Studios. Men's voices shouted.

I felt her hand on my arm as she shoved me down a dark alley. We ran blindly as the siren continued to moan into the night.

"Here!"

She pulled me into a dark doorway. For a brief moment her flashlight made a puddle of light, then turned off. She pulled me down behind a big wooden crate.

We heard racing, heavy footsteps go by. We heard men shouting to each other. Someone began to blow a shrill whistle that set my nerves jangling.

"Come on!"

If it hadn't been for her, I would never have got out of the place. She was terribly cool and controlled. She steered me through the

47

dark alleys. She seemed to know when we were about to run into danger and when it was clear to go ahead.

As we ran past the endless buildings and the vast Studio sheds, the whistles and the voices grew fainter, and at last, panting, we stopped in the shadow of a building to listen.

There was silence now except the still moaning siren.

"We've got to get out of here before the cops arrive," Rima said. "You killed him!

"Oh, shut up! We can get over the wall at the end of this alley."

I went with her until we came to a ten-foot wall. We paused beside it and looked up at it.

"Help me up.

I took her foot in both my hands and heaved her up. She swung one leg over the wall, bending low and stared down into the darkness.

"It's okay. Can you get up?"

I walked back, ran at the wall, jumped and grabbed at the top. I got a grip, hung for a moment, then heaved myself up. We both rolled over the wall and dropped onto the dirt road that ran alongside the Studio.

We walked quickly to the main road. Along this road was parked a line of cars belonging to people in a night club across the way.

"There should be a bus in five minutes or so," Rima said.

I heard the approaching sound of police sirens.

Rima grabbed my arm and shoved me to a Skyliner Ford.

"Get in-quick!"

I slid in and she followed.

She had just time to close the door when two police cars went storming past, heading for the main entrance to the Studio.

"We'll wait here," Rima said. "There'll be more coming. They mustn't see us on the street."

This made sense although I was aching to get away.

"Larry!" Rima said, disgust in her voice. "I should have known he would get it all wrong. They must bank the money or put it in a safe when they close down."

"Do you realise you've killed a man?" I said. "They can send us to the gas chamber. You mad bitch! I wish I had never had anything to do with you!"

"It was in self-defence," she said hotly. "I had to do it!"

"It wasn't! You shot him down in cold blood. You shot him twice!"

"I would have been a fool to let him shoot me, wouldn't I? He had a gun in his hand. It was self-defence!"

"It was murder!"

"Oh, shut up!"

"I'm through with you. I never want to see you again so long as I live!"

"You're yellow! You wanted the money as much as I did! You wanted to make money out of me!. Now, when things turn sour ..."

"You call killing a man turning sour?"

"Oh, quiet down!"

I sat still, my hands gripping the steering wheel. I was panic stricken. I told myself I must have been out of my mind to have got mixed up with her. If I got away I would go home and I would start my studies again. I would never do a bad thing again so long as I lived.

We heard more sirens. Another police car packed with plain clothes men went past, and a few seconds later, an ambulance.

"That's the end of the procession," Rima said. "Let's go.

She got out of the car and I followed her.

We walked fast to the bus stop. After two or three minutes the bus arrived.

We sat at the back. No one paid us any attention. Rima smoked, staring out of the window. As we came down the main road to the waterfront, she began to sneeze.

CHAPTER FIVE

I

Soon after seven o'clock the next morning, I woke out of a restless sleep, and staring up at the ceiling, I thought back on the previous night. I felt pretty bad.

I had had only three or four hours' sleep. Most of the night I had thought of the guard and how Rima had shot him.

She had gone to her room when we had got back, and I had heard her snivelling and sneezing for an hour until I thought the sound would drive me crazy. Then I heard her go out and I guessed she was going to hunt for some sucker to buy her a shot.

I was asleep when she came in. I was aware of her door shutting but I was so tired, I turned over and went off to sleep again.

Now, lying in bed, with the sun coming around the edges of the blind, I wondered what I had best do. I had to leave town. I didn't dare stay here any longer. I would see Rusty, borrow the fare from him, and I'd leave this morning.

There was a train out around eleven o'clock.

49

My bedroom door opened abruptly and Rima came in. She was dressed, wearing her red shirt and her skin tight jeans. She looked pale and her eyes were glittering unnaturally. She had had her shot all right.

She stood at the foot of the bed, looking at me.

"What do you want?" I said. "Get out of here!"

"I'm going to the Studios. Aren't you coming?"

"Are you crazy? I wouldn't go back there for all the money in the world."

She wrinkled her nose at me, her eyes contemptuous.

"I'm not going to pass up that job. If I do, it'll be the last I'll get. What are you going to do then?"

"I'm leaving town. Have you forgotten you killed a man last night or is it just one of those things you can brush off?"

She smiled.

"They think you did it."

That brought me bolt upright in bed.

"Me? What do you mean?"

"Relax. No one killed anyone. He's not dead."

I threw off the sheet and swung my feet to the floor.

"How do you know?"

"It's in the paper."

"Where is it?"

"It was outside one of the rooms."

"Well, don't stand there! Get it!"

"It's gone now."

I felt like strangling her.

"They really say he isn't dead?"

She nodded, her eyes bored.

"Yes".

I reached for a cigarette and lit it with a shaking hand. The surge of relief that ran through me left me breathless.

"Where do you get that line about me killing him?" I demanded.

"He's given the cops a description of you. They're looking for a man with a scarred face."

"Don't give me that! It was you who shot him!"

"He didn't see me! He saw you!"

"He knows I didn't shoot him," I said, trying to keep my voice down. "He knows I was facing the wall when you shot at him! He must know I didn't do it!"

She shrugged her shoulders indifferently.

"All I know is the police are looking for a man with a scar. You'd better watch out."

By now I was ready to hit the ceiling.

"Get me a paper! Do you hear? Get me a paper!"

"Stop shouting. Do you want everyone to hear you? I've got to catch the bus to the Studio. Maybe you'd better stay here and not show yourself."

I grabbed hold of her arm.

"Where did you get the gun from?"

"It belonged to Wilbur. Let go of me!" She jerked free. "Don't lose your nerve. I've been in worse jams than this. If you keep under cover for a couple of days, you'll be all right. Then you can get out of town, but don't try to go before."

"Once they get a lead on me, this will be the first place they'll come to!"

"Oh, quiet down!" Her tone of contempt maddened me. "You're yellow. Keep your nerve and you'll be all right. Just relax, can't you? You're boring me."

I caught her by the throat and slammed her against the wall. Then I slapped her face: bang! . bang! . bang! I wasn't proud of myself for hitting her, but I had to. She was so rotten I had no answer to her attitude but to hit her.

I let go of her and stood away from her, panting.

"I'm scared!" I said. "I'm scared because I have some decency left in me. You! You have nothing. You're rotten through and through! I wish I never had anything to do with you! Get out!"

She leaned against the wall, her face where I had hit her red as fire, her eyes glowing with hate.

"I won't forget that, you skunk," she said. "I've a lot to remember you by. One of these days, I'll even the score. I hope he dies and I hope you go to the gas chamber!"

I threw the bedroom door open.

"Get out!" I yelled at her.

She went out and I slammed the door after her.

For a long moment I stood motionless, trying to control my breathing. Then I went over to the mirror and stared at my white, frightened face. I looked at the thin scar that ran down the side of my jaw. If the guard, had described that to the police I was cooked.

I was stiff with panic. My one thought now was to get away and go home, but if the police were already looking for me, it would be asking for trouble to show myself on the streets in daylight.

I heard Carrie come thumping up the stairs. I opened the door.

"Do me a favour," I said. "I'm staying in today. Get me a paper, will you?"

She looked sharply at me.

"I ain't got time, Mr. Jeff. I've got work to do."

"It's important. Can't you borrow one for me?" I had to make an effort to keep calm. "Try and get me one, Carrie."

"I'll see. Are you sick?"

51

"I'm not feeling too bright. Get that paper for me."

She nodded and went off downstairs.

I got back into bed, lit another cigarette and waited. I had to wait half an hour, and by then I was in a terrible state of nerves. Then I heard her lumbering up the stairs again. I jumped out of bed and went to the door.

She pushed a paper at me and a cup of coffee.

"Thanks, Carrie."

"The missus was reading it."

"That's okay. Thanks."

I shut the door, set down the coffee and looked at the front page of the paper.

The usual war headlines took priority. The date was August 5th, 1945. Super Fortresses, so the headlines told me, had been continually flying over Japan, plastering eleven Japanese cities with leaflets, warning the people of intensive bombing to come.

The threat to Japan didn't interest me. What I was hunting for was a threat to myself.

I found it finally on the back page.

A guard at the Pacific Studios had surprised an intruder and been shot, the report said. The guard, an ex-policeman, well liked when on the force, was now in the Los Angeles State hospital. He had given the police a description of the gunman before lapsing into a coma. The police were hunting for a man with a scar on his face.

That was all, but it was bad enough.

I felt so bad, I had to sit on the bed, my legs refusing to support me.

Maybe this guard was going to die after all.

After a while, I got dressed. I had a feeling that I might have to make a bolt for it, and I had the urge to be ready. I packed my suitcase, and I checked my money. I had only ten dollars and fifty cents left in the world.

Then I sat by the window, watching the street below.

A little after midday, I saw a police car pull up at the far end of the street and four plain clothes men spill out. The sight of them set my heart hammering so violently I could scarcely breathe.

In this street were four rooming-houses. The detectives split up and walked rapidly towards the various houses.

The one who headed for mine was a big man with a pork pie hat on the back of his head and a dead cigar butt gripped between his teeth.

I watched him walk up the steps and I heard the bell ring as he thumbed the bell push.

I left the window and went out onto the landing. I looked down over the banisters, three flights into the hall.

I saw Carrie cross the hall and heard her open the front door.

I heard the hard cop voice bark,"City police. We're looking for a man, youngish with a scar on his face. Anyone like that living here?"

I had my hands on the banister rail. I gripped the rail so tightly, the heat of my hands made the varnish sticky.

"A scar?" Carrie sounded bewildered. "No, sir. No one is here with any scar."

I leaned against the rail, blessing her.

"You sure about that?"

"Yes, sir. I'm sure. I'd know if there was anyone here with a scar. There ain't."

"This guy is wanted for murder. You still sure?"

"No one living here with a scar, sir."

Wanted for murder!

So he had died!

I went back to my room and lay on the bed. I was cold, sweating and shaking.

Time stood still.

I lay there, sweating it out, maybe for ten or maybe twenty minutes, then there came a hesitant knock on the door.

"Come in."

Carrie opened the door and stared at me. Her fat, lined face was anxious.

"There was a police officer..."

"I was listening. Come in, Carrie, and shut the door."

She came in, closing the door.

I sat up on the bed.

"Thanks. It's nothing to do with me, but you saved me some trouble."

I went over to the dressing-table for my wallet.

"That cop could have made things tricky for me," I went on, taking out a five-dollar bill. "I want you to have this, Carrie."

She wouldn't take it.

"I don't want it, Mr. Jeff. I lied because we are friends."

I had a sudden wave of emotion that nearly made me cry. I sat abruptly on the bed.

"You're in trouble, aren't you?" she said, looking searchingly at me.

"Yes. I didn't have anything to do with the shooting, Carrie. I wouldn't shoot anyone."

"You don't have to tell me. You stay quiet. Would you like a cup of coffee?"

"I don't want anything, thanks."

53

"Don't worry. I'll get you a paper later on," she opened the door, then paused. "She's gone." She nodded in the direction of Rima's door.

"She told me."

"Good riddance. You take it easy," and she went away.

Soon after five o'clock, she came into my room and dropped the evening paper on the bed. She looked pale and bothered, and she gave me a long, uneasy stare before she went out.

As soon as she had shut the door, I grabbed the paper.

The guard had died without coming out of his coma.

The paragraph was small beside the war headlines, but the words hit me like a punch in the face.

The police were still looking for a youngish man with a scar on his face: an arrest was expected at any moment.

As soon as it was dark, I told myself, I would get out. The thought of staying in this box of a room was hard to take, but I knew I didn't dare go onto the streets as long as it was light.

Leaving the room, I went down the stairs to the pay booth and called Rusty.

It was good to hear the sound of his hard, rough voice.

I'm in trouble, Rusty. Will you come over to my place when it's dark?"

"Who do you imagine is going to keep the bar open if I do that?" he growled.

I hadn't thought of that.

"Maybe I could come to you......

"How bad is the trouble?"

"As bad as it can be."

He must have picked up the panic in my voice for he said soothingly, "Keep your shirt on. I'll get Sam to handle it. When it's dark, huh?"

"Not before."

"Okay. I'll be over," and he hung up.

I went back to my room and waited. It was a long wait, and I was in a pretty bad way by the time the sun went down over the bay and the lights went on in the honky-tonk bars and on the gambling ships. At least there now seemed safety out there in the growing darkness.

A little after nine o'clock I saw Rusty's Oldsmobile come around the corner, and I went down the stairs and had the front door open as he came up the steps.

We climbed the three flights of stairs in silence. It was only when he was in my room and I had shut the door that the tension in me eased a little.

54

"Thanks, Rusty, for coming."

He sat on the bed, his fat, blue jowled face shiny with sweat, his eyes anxious.

"What's the trouble? That girl?"

"Yes."

I picked up the evening paper and gave it to him, pointing to the paragraph with a shaking finger.

He read it, his face screwed up, his expression blank.

Then he looked up and stared at me.

"For Pete's sake! You didn't do it, did you?"

"No, but she did. I must have been out of my mind. I wanted five thousand dollars for her cure. She told me we could find the money in the casting director's office. I fell for it. We went out there, broke in, but there was no money. The guard caught me. She was behind the desk, out of sight. She shot him." I sat on the upright chair and hid my face in my hands. "I was against the wall, with my back turned to him. Listen, Rusty, I swear I didn't do it."

He put the paper down, took out a crumpled pack of cigarettes, shook one out into his large hand and lit it.

"So you're in trouble. Well, I warned you, didn't I? I told you she'd be a load of grief to you."

"You told me."

"Well? What are you going to do?"

"I want to get out of here. I want to go home."

"That's about the first sensible thing you have said since I've known you." He put his hand inside his coat and took out a shabby wallet. "Here you are: as soon as I heard the state you were in, I raided the till."

He offered me five twenty dollar bills.

"I don't want all that, Rusty."

"Take it and shut up."

"No. All I want is my fare home. It'll be ten bucks. I'm not taking any more."

He got to his feet, cramming the bills back into his wallet.

"You'd better not travel from L.A. Station. They may have the joint pegged out. I'll drive you to 'Frisco. You can get a train from there."

"If they stop us and find me with you..."

"Forget it! Come on: let's go."

He went to the door and started down the stairs. Picking up my suitcase, I followed him.

In the lobby, Carrie was waiting.

"I'm going home, Carrie," I said.

Rusty moved on into the street, leaving us together.

"Here." I offered her my last two five-dollar bills. "I want you to have these . . ."

She took one of the bills.

"That'll take care of the room, Mr. Jeff. You keep the rest. You'll need it. Good luck."

"I didn't do it, Carrie. No matter what they say, I didn't do it."

Her smile was weary as she patted my arm.

"Good luck, Mr. Jeff."

I went out into the darkness and got into the Oldsmobile. As I slammed the door, Rusty shot the car away from the kerb.

We had been driving for ten minutes or so in silence, when I said, "It's a funny thing, Rusty, but all I can think of now is to get home. I've learned my lesson. If I get away with this mess, I'm going to start my studies again. I'm through with this kind of life-through with it for good."

Rusty grunted.

"It's about time."

"You heard her sing. She had a voice in a million. If only she hadn't been a junky..."

"If she hadn't been a junky, you would never have met her. That's the way it is. If you ever see her again, you run for your life."

"I'll do that. I hope I'll never see her again."

We reached San Francisco around three o'clock in the morning. Rusty parked by the station while I waited in the car, he went to check on the trains.

When he came back, I could see he was worried.

"There's a train to Holland City just after eight: eight ten," he said. "There are two cops at the booking office. Maybe they aren't looking for you, but they're there. You can by-pass them. I bought your ticket."

I took the ticket and put it in my wallet.

"Thanks. You leave me now, Rusty. I'll go and sit in a cafe and wait. I'll pay you back. You've been a real pal to me."

"You go home and settle down to a job of work. I don't want the money back. You keep clear of Los Angeles from now on. The way to pay me back is to settle down and do a real job of work."

We sat side by side in his car, smoking, dozing and talking while the hours crept by.

A little after seven o'clock, Rusty said, "We have time for a coffee, then you can get off."

We left the car and walked over to a coffee bar. We had coffee and doughnuts.

56

The time came when my train was due. I took Rusty's hand in mine and squeezed it.

"Thanks."

"Forget it. Let me know how you make out."

He gave me a slap on my shoulder, then walked fast to his car.

I walked into the station, holding my handkerchief to my face to hide my scar.

No one paid any attention to me.

. Long before the train got me home, something happened that made the murder of a film studio guard no news at all: an event that had such a tremendous impact that the hunt for a man with a scar on his face became something of no importance.

An atomic bomb was dropped on Hiroshima.

Under cover of this momentous news, I got home in safety.

By the time Japan had surrendered, I was back in college. By the time the world began the tricky business of peace making, I was qualified as a consulting engineer: two years exactly from the first time I had met Rima.

I wasn't to meet her again for another eleven years.

PART TWO

CHAPTER ONE

I

A LOT can happen in eleven years.

Looking back on those years, I can say now that they were the most exciting and most invigorating of my life.

The one black spot was when my father died, two years after I had qualified as a consulting engineer. He died from a heart attack while working in the bank: the way he would have wanted to die if he had had the choice. He left me five thousand dollars and the house which I sold. With this for capital, plus my qualifications as a trained engineer, I went into partnership with Jack Osborne.

Jack had been in my battle unit when I had gone to the Philippines. We had landed on the beaches of Okinawa together. He was five years older than I was, and had completed his training as an engineer before he had gone to war. He was thick set, short and tubby with sandy coloured hair, going thin on top and a brick red face, covered with freckles.

But what a ball of fire! He had a capacity for work that left me standing. He could work twenty hours of the day, snatch four hours' sleep, and then start again with the same dynamic drive.

It was my good luck that he came to Holland City to look me up around the time when I had five thousand dollars from my father's estate.

Jack had been in town three days before he called on me, and during that time he had talked to people, summed up the city, and had decided this was the place where a consulting engineer could make a living.

Then he breezed into my one-room apartment, put out a hard, rough hand and grinned at me.

"Jeff," he said,"I've looked this place over, and this is where I'm setting up my flag. How about you and me going into partnership?"

So we set up in business as Osborne and Halliday.

Halliday was my father's name. I had taken my mother's name of Gordon when I had gone to Hollywood as I had been unsure of myself and I had had an instinctive feeling that I might run into something that I wouldn't like to get back to my father. One of those odd instincts that happen and that pay off.

For the next three years we didn't do much except sit around in our one-room office and wait and hope. If we hadn't had some money behind us we would have starved, but between us we managed to get by, but it was tight living. We shared a room in a rooming-house; we cooked our own meals. We did our own typing. We ran the office without the usual girl help.

Then, out of the blue, we got an offer to put up a block of apartment houses down by the river. The competition was blue murder, but we went at it like soldiers. We cut the costs to the bone and we got the job. Financially, we didn't get much out of it, but at least it showed those interested what we could do.

Slowly we began to get other jobs, not as cut-throat but nearly as bad. It took us two more years to crawl out of the red into the black. Don't imagine it was easy. It was tooth, claw and no holds barred, but we came out of it, and finally into the open.

Jack and I worked well as a team. He handled the outside work while I looked after the office. By now we were able to afford help. We hired Clara Collins, a thin, middle-aged spinster who looked on us as a couple of crazy kids, but who ran the office with an efficiency that more than covered her cost.

After we had been in business six years, we began to get a lot of private building: houses, bungalows, petrol stations, and even a small movie house, but we weren't getting any civic building and that's where the big money lay.

I decided to cultivate the mayor. His name was Henry Mathison. I had met him a couple of times and he seemed pretty easy to get along with. His son had been killed in the Philippines and when he learned Jack and I had fought out there, he was friendly, but he wasn't friendly enough to throw any business our way.

Every civic project that came up we sent in estimates, but we never heard further. The established engineers always got the jobs: three firms that had been in Holland City for over, twenty years.

It was while I was trying to find a real point of contact with the mayor that I met Sarita Fleming.

Sarita was in charge of Holland City's Public Library. Her people lived in New York. She had taken some kind of degree in Literature and had been offered this job which she had jumped at as her mother and she didn't get along together. She had been at the library two years before I wandered in, looking for information about Mathison.

After I had explained to her exactly what I wanted, Sarita couldn't have been more helpful. She knew quite a lot about the mayor. She told me he was keen on duck shooting, was a good amateur cine operator and he liked classical music. Duck shooting and cine camera work were out of my field, but classical music put me back in the fight. Sarita said he was wildly enthusiastic about Chopin's piano music.

She mentioned she had four tickets for a Chopin recital that was being held at the City Hall with Stefan Askenase at the piano, one of the greatest Chopin-exponents in the world. She had been selling the tickets in the library and she had kept four of them back just in case. She knew Mathison hadn't got a ticket and wouldn't it be an idea for me to ask him to go with me?

The idea was so sound I looked up and stared at her, and this was the first time I really saw her.

She was tall and slim with a good figure. She wore a simple grey dress that showed off her figure to advantage. She had nice brown eyes; brown hair, parted in the middle and pulled back to form a coil of silky hair on the nape of her neck.

She wasn't pretty, but there was something about her that excited me. Just looking at her, I had a feeling that she was the only possible woman I could live with, wouldn't grow tired of, and who would make me happy.

It was an odd feeling. It came to me in a flash, and I knew then that if I was going to continue with my streak of good luck, before very long, she would be my wife.

I asked her if she would make up the fourth of the party: Mathison, his wife, she and me, and she accepted.

Jack was enthusiastic when he heard what I was planning.

"Thank the Lord I have a partner with some culture," he said. "Take the old fellow to Chopin and impress him. Maybe he'll throw some business our way if he thinks you and he have the same taste."

I called up Mathison and asked him if he and his wife would care to join me and a friend for the concert, and he jumped at it.

As it worked out, it wasn't Chopin nor I who impressed Mathison, it was Sarita. She made a big hit with him, and not only with him, but his wife as well.

The evening had been a success.

As we shook hands before parting, he said,"It's time we saw something of you at the office, young man. Look in tomorrow. I want you to meet Merrill Webb."

Webb was the City's planning officer. He was the guy who handed out the jobs. Without his say-so, you got nowhere. I hadn't even met him.

I was feeling on top of the world as I drove Sarita to her apartment. I knew I had her to thank for this opening, and I asked her if she would dine with me the night aft.. next and she said she would.

The next morning I went to the City H? and met Webb. He was a lean, dried up, stoop-shouldered man in his late fifties. He talked to me casually, asking about my training and Jack's training, what we had done so far and stuff like that. He didn't seem particularly interested. Finally, he shook hands and said that if he had something he thought we could handle he would let me know.

I was a little damped by this. I had had hopes that he would have given us something to work on right-away.

Jack said he wasn't surprised.

"You keep after Mathison. He's the guy who tells Webb what to do. Keep after Mathison, and sooner or later, we'll land in the gravy."

From then on, I saw a lot of Sarita. We went out every other night, and after a couple of weeks I knew I was in love with her and wanted to marry her.

I was now making a reasonable living; not a great deal, but enough to support a wife. I saw no reason why we should wait, providing she was willing to throw her lot in with me, so I asked her.

There was no hesitation when she said yes.

When I told Jack he leaned back in his desk chair and beamed at me.

"Boy! Am I glad! It's high time one of us became respectable! And what a girl! I'll tell you something: if you hadn't got there first, I would have grabbed her. The best, Jeff. I'm not kidding. That girl's solid gold right through. I know a sterling character when I see one: she's it."

Don't imagine during these years I hadn't thought of Rima nor of the guard she had murdered. Don't imagine there weren't times when I would wake up in the middle of the night from a nightmare when I imagined Rima was in the room, looking at me. But as the years went by, and the thing became something in the dim past, I began to feel confident that it was in the past and would remain that way.

I had thought a lot about it before I had asked Sarita to be my wife. Finally, I decided it was a risk I could afford to take. No one knew me as Gordon. I had grown up and altered considerably since I was in Los Angeles, although the scar persisted and so did the drooping eyelid. I felt I had seen the last of Rima and the last of my past.

We were married towards the end of the year. As a wedding present we got the job of building the new wing to the State hospital. It was a nice job and it made us money. That was Mathison's influence.

61

It enabled Jack to move into a three room penthouse and Sarita and I into a four-room, more modest apartment in the better district. It allowed both of us to buy better cars and we entertained more.

Life seemed pretty good. We felt we had at last arrived. Then one morning the telephone bell rang and Mathison came on the line.

"Come over here right away, Jeff," he said. "Drop everything. There's something I want to talk to you about."

This abrupt summons left me wondering, but I dropped everything, told Clara I'd be back when she saw me, told her to tell Jack who was out on a construction job where to find me, and hot footed over to City Hall.

Mathison and Webb were together in Mathison's office.

Sit down, boy," Mathison said, waving to a chair. "You've heard about the Holland bridge?"

"Why, sure."

"This morning we have got it fixed. We have the money, and now we're going to build."

This was a project that every construction engineer in the county and a lot outside the county had been waiting for. It was to take the up-town traffic out of Holland City across the river. This was the big job. The estimated cost ran into six million dollars.

My heart started to thump. Mathison wouldn't have called me just to tell me this piece of news. I waited, looking at him and then at Webb.

Mathison grinned at me.

"Do you think you and Osborne could build it?"

"We can build it."

"I've talked it over with Webb. Of course it'll have to go before the committee, but if you come up with the right figures and you can convince the bone heads you can build the bridge within a year, I think I can persuade them to let you go ahead. You'll have all the boys up against you, but I'm going to lean over backwards just a little and if your price isn't right, I'm going to tell you so before the committee sees your estimates: that way you should get the job."

For the next thirty days I scarcely saw Sarita.

Jack and I slaved in the office from eight o'clock in the morning until sometimes as late as three o'clock the next morning.

This was our big chance to break into Big-time and we weren't taking any chances.

Finally, the pressure got so tough, I asked Sarita to come into the office to handle the typing so Clara could spend her time on the calculating machine, getting out figures for us.

The four of us slaved.

At the end of thirty days we had the estimates and the plan of operation ready.

I went around to Mathison and handed the document over. He said he would let me know, and that was that.

We waited three long, nerve-racking months, then he telephoned me and told me to come over.

"It's okay, boy," he said, coming over to shake me by the hand. "The job's yours. I'm not saying I didn't have a fight to convince some of them, but your figures were right, and you had half the committee on your side to start with. You can go right ahead. Talk to Webb. There'll be another meeting tomorrow. I want you and Osborne to be there."

That happened exactly ten years, eleven months and two weeks since last I saw Rima.

II

I hadn't considered what the building of a six million dollar bridge would mean until Joe Creedy, the City's Public Relations Officer, breezed into our office and told me.

We had celebrated of course: just our own private celebration with Sarita, Jack, Clara and myself. We had gone to the best restaurant in Holland City and had had a champagne dinner. As far as I was concerned the celebrations were over and we had now to get down to the business of building the bridge, but Creedy had other ideas.

Creedy was a big, broad-shouldered man with a heavy, serious face and a likeable manner. He paced the office while Jack and I sat at our desks and listened to him.

"There'll be a civic banquet on Saturday," he told us. "You two will be guests of honour. One of you will have to make a speech."

Jack grinned broadly and jerked his thumb at me.

"You're the boy, Jeff. I wouldn't know how to make a speech."

"I'll write it," Creedy said. "I don't care who delivers it so long as it gets delivered. On Sunday at three o'clock I've fixed it for you two to appear on television. I'll pick you up here and take you over to the studio."

"Television?" I said and I felt a little stab of uneasiness. "What do we want to be on television for?"

Creedy smiled patiently at me.

"We're spending six million dollars of this city's money," he said "The public are entitled to see the two guys who are spending their money. There's nothing to it. I'll ask the usual corny questions and you'll give me the usual corny answers. We'll have a scale model of the bridge prepared and you explain how you're going to build it."

I was now beginning to get even more uneasy. My past was beginning to come alive in my mind. I told myself not to panic. "After all, the television hook-up covered the country: we were a long way from Los Angeles.

"I'm trying to get *Life* to do an article about the bridge," Creedy went on. "They're biting. It would be a fine thing for the city to get a coverage from *Life*."

My uneasiness sparked into panic. Coverage in Life was world wide. I would have to make sure there would be no photograph of me in the magazine.

Jack said happily,"Sounds as if we have become a couple of famous people, Jeff. It's about time. We've worked hard enough."

Creedy took out his notebook.

"You're famous all right. Let's have some dope about yourselves. I want to prepare the TV interview. Let's get the basic facts: where you were born, who your parents were, what your training was, your war service, what you've done since the war, your future plans: that kind of junk."

Jack gave him the information, and while I listened I began to sweat. I had to cover up on the time I had spent in Los Angeles.

When it came my turn, it was easy until I came to my return home from hospital.

Creedy said,"You began your studies again, and then you suddenly quit: is that right?"

"Yes." I didn't want to tell him any lies so I picked my way carefully. "I couldn't settle to work. I left college after three months, and for a while I just kicked around."

"Is that so." He showed interest. "Where did you get to?"

"All over. I just loafed around and did nothing."

He looked sharply at me

"How did you earn a living?"

"I did a job here: a job there."

Jack was now looking interested.

"You never told me," he said. "I thought you had been in the engineering racket all the time."

"For a year or so I bummed around."

"This could make for colour," Creedy said. "Where did you get to? What kind of jobs did you do?"

This was now dangerous. I had to kill it.

"I'd rather not go into that. Suppose we skip it if it's all the same to you."

Creedy stared at me, then shrugged.

"Sure. What are you going to do with the money you'll make out of the bridge?"

I relaxed. That was an easy one.

"Buy a house I guess. I might even build one."

Creedy closed his notebook.

"Well, I guess that'll hold it for the moment. Don't forget the banquet on Saturday."

When he had gone, we got down to work again. There was so much to do, I didn't have time to think about this unexpected publicity until I was driving home.

Then I began to worry.

I now began to think of Rima not as someone in the dim past, but someone who could come into my present and my future.

Suppose she spotted my photograph in the newspapers and recognised me? What would she do? It depended on the state she was in. Maybe by now she had had a cure and was living a decent, normal life. Maybe she was no longer alive. I told myself to quit worrying. She was in the past, and with any luck she would remain in the past.

Sarita had dinner waiting for me when I walked into our three-room apartment.

The sight of her waiting by a roaring fire, a shaker of dry Martinis on the table, and an atmosphere in the room that can only come from a woman who really cares for her man, quieted my uneasiness.

I held her close to me, my face against hers, and I was thankful she was mine.

"You look tired, Jeff. How has it been going?"

"Pretty hectic. There's still an awful lot to do." I kissed her and then dropped into the lounging chair. It's good to be home. There's to be a banquet on Saturday night in our honour, and Jack and I have to go on television on Sunday."

She poured two cocktails.

"Seems I have married a famous man."

"So it seems, but I know I have you to thank for it." I raised my glass to her. "You began the bridge."

"No-it was Chopin."

After dinner we sat by the fire. I was in the armchair and Sarita on the floor, her head against my knee.

"Pretty soon," I said. "we're going to have some money to burn. Creedy asked me what I was going to do with it. I said maybe I'd build a house. Would that be an idea?"

"We wouldn't have to build it, Jeff. I've seen a place that is exactly what we want."

"You've seen it? Where?"

"It's that little cottage up on Simeon's Hill. It's owned by Mr. Terrell. Last year he and his wife invited me out there for dinner. Oh, Jeff! It has everything, and it's not too big."

"What makes you think it's in the market?"

"I met Mr. Terrell yesterday. He is taking his wife to live in Miami. She needs the sun. Of course it is for you to decide, but you must see it. I'm sure you'll love it."

"If it's good enough for you, it's good enough for me. You don't know what he wants for it?"

"I'll call him tomorrow and ask him."

I wasn't the only one of the firm who was planning to spend some money.

When I got into the office the next morning, Jack told me he had ordered a Thunderbird.

"Boy! Am I going to cut a dash!" he exclaimed. "What's money for unless you spend it? And another thing: it's time I had some new furniture. Could you persuade Sarita to do something about it? I haven't time to look after that myself."

"Have dinner with us tonight; and persuade her yourself. There's talk about us buying Terrell's cottage on Simeon's Hill. Sarita is making inquiries this morning."

He grinned at me.

"We've arrived, pal! I'm getting a big bang out of this." He gathered up a heap of papers and crammed them into his brief case. "I've got to get off. See you tonight."

I spent the morning interviewing contractors and working out costs. While I was eating a sandwich lunch, Creedy blew in with a couple of guys, one of them carrying a Rolleiflex camera and a flash equipment. The sight of the camera brought back my uneasiness.

"These boys are from *Life*," Creedy said. "I've given them most of the dope. They just want some photograph of you working at your desk. Osborne around?"

I said Jack was on the site.

As I was speaking the camera man let off his flash.

"Look, I don't want my photograph in your paper," I said. "I..."

"He's shy," Creedy said, laughing. "Of course he does! Who wouldn't want his photograph in *Life*!"

The camera man went on popping off his flashlight. I realised there was nothing I could do about it. I did put my hand up to my face to cover my scar, but the other fellow then showed interest in it.

"Did you get that during the war, Mr. Halliday?"

"Yes."

"We'd like a shot of it. Would you turn your face a little to the left?"

"I don't want it advertised," I said, curtly. "If it's all right with you two, I have to get on with my job."

I saw Creedy looking at me, frowning, but I didn't care.

The two guys exchanged glances, then the camera man strolled to the door. The other one said, "You were at Holland City's Plastic Hospital, weren't you, Mr. Halliday?"

"Yes."

"Had a tough time?"

"So did the others."

He grinned sympathetically.

"I hear you play the piano. Is that right?"

"When I have the time."

I had forgotten about the camera man and had taken my hand off my scar. The flash told me he hadn't forgotten me. He moved out of the office, and the other fellow shook hands, said he had all he wanted and then he and Creedy went away.

That spoilt my day's work. I kept thinking of the photographs that would appear in *Life*. I kept wondering who of those I had known in Los Angeles would recognise Jeff Halliday as Jeff Gordon and wonder.

I managed to shake off my mood of depression by the time Jack and I got home.

Sarita was excited. She had talked to Mr. Terrell who had told her he was leaving in two months' time, and if we wanted the cottage we could have it.

Sarita had arranged for us to go out there after dinner and inspect it.

During dinner, Jack talked to her about how he wanted his penthouse furnished and Sarita promised to get it organised for him.

The three of us drove out to Simeon's Hill. As soon as I saw the cottage, perched on the hill with a big garden and a view over the river, I fell for it.

But at the back of my mind now was a growing fear so I didn't enthuse all that much about it.

Inside, it was as perfect as Sarita had claimed it to be. It was exactly what we wanted: three bedrooms, a big lounge, a study, a kitchen with every push button device you could think of, and a built-in bar on the patio as well as a big brick oven for barbecues.

The price was thirty thousand and it was cheap.

"Boy!" Jack exclaimed. "This is the place for you two! It's as perfect as you could find anywhere."

He was right, but something warned me to be cautious. I asked if Mr. Terrell would let me think it over. He said he would give me a week to make up my mind.

When Jack had left us and we were getting ready for bed, Sarita asked me if I didn't like the cottage.

"It's fine, but I don't want to rush into it. Suppose you go to Harcourt and see if he has anything like it on the market. We may as well take a look before closing with Terrell's place. We have a week."

The next two days passed fast enough. I was working to capacity and Sarita was house hunting. She didn't find anything, and I could see she was a little impatient with me for wanting her to look. She was so sold on Terrell's place she just couldn't believe there could be anything to beat it.

She brought home a copy of Life. There was a biggish picture of me, sitting at my desk with the drooping eyelid and the scar very much in evidence.

The caption ran as follows:

"War Veteran Jeff Halliday plans to build his own house after building Holland City's six million dollar bridge. A good amateur pianist, he plays Chopin's Nocturnes as a relaxation after a sixteen hour stint at his desk."

That caption really bothered me. It was a complete giveaway if anyone who knew me as Jeff Gordon saw it, together with the photograph.

The following night was the banquet. It was an ordeal for me, but I got through it without disgracing myself.

Mathison said a lot of nice things about Jack and myself. He said the city had every confidence in us. He had watched us come up in the world, and he was sure we were going far, and that we would make a splendid bridge, and a lot more of that kind of guff.

I looked across at Sarita while Mathison was sounding off. She was dewy eyed and very proud. We smiled at each other.. It was one of the highlights of my life.

Sunday was the television date.

Sarita didn't come to the studio. She said she preferred to watch me on our set at home.

It went off all right. Creedy's idea of having a scale model of the bridge was a good one. It allowed both Jack and myself to explain just how we were going to handle the job, and it proved to the taxpayers that a job of this size couldn't be built without spending a great deal of money.

During the interview, Creedy said,"It's no secret that you two are getting a hundred and twenty thousand dollar fee for this job. What are you going to do with the money?"

Jack said,"After I've given most of it to the tax collector, I'm buying a car."

Creedy looked at me.

"You, I understand, Mr. Halliday, are planning a new home."
"That's right," I said.

"Are you building it yourself?"

"I haven't decided yet."

"He has enough to do handling the bridge without thinking of building a house," Jack broke in, and the interview broke up in general laughter.

As soon as the camera swung away from us, Creedy opened a bottle of champagne and we had drinks. I was itching to get home to Sarita, but I couldn't break away too soon.

"Well, boys, I guess the bridge is launched," Creedy said. "Now, go ahead and build it."

We shook hands with him.

One of the technicians came over.

"You're wanted on the telephone, Mr. Halliday."

"I bet that's his wife calling to tell him how handsome he looked," Jack said. "I'll meet you downstairs."

He and Creedy walked out of the studio.

For a moment I hesitated, then aware that the technician was looking curiously at me, I went to the telephone and picked up the receiver.

I had an instinctive feeling who was calling. I was right.

"Hello," Rima said. "I've been watching your little performance. Congratulations."

I felt cold sweat start out on my forehead.

People were buzzing around me. I had to be careful what I said. "Thanks."

"So you're a rich man now."

"I can't talk now."

"I didn't expect you to. I'll meet you in the lobby of the Calloway Hotel at ten o'clock. You had better be there."

I heard her break the connection, and slowly I replaced the receiver.

I took out my handkerchief and wiped my sweating face. I knew I was as pale as death and I was shaking.

"Anything wrong, Mr. Halliday?"

"No. It's all right."

"Maybe the heat from the lamps. You look pretty bad."

"I'll get out into the open air. I'll be okay."

"Do you want me to come with you?"

"No... no thanks. I'll be all right. It was just the heat."

I went out of the studio and down the stairs to where Jack and Creedy were waiting.

CHAPTER TWO

I

I HAD trouble finding the Calloway Hotel. When finally I ran it to earth it turned out to be one of those dingy room-by-the-hour joints that are scattered along the waterfront of the Eastside of the river, and which are being continually closed down by the police, and as regularly opened up again under new management.

After I had dropped Creedy at a restaurant where he was to meet his wife and Jack at his apartment, it was too late for me to go home and then recross the city to meet Rima by ten.

So I called Sarita and told her I had to go to the office as Creedy wanted some figures for an article he was writing. I said I would be having a snack with him and I wasn't sure what time I would get home. I felt bad lying to her, but this was something I couldn't tell her.

I walked into the lobby of the Calloway Hotel a few minutes after ten.

There was an old white haired negro behind the reception desk. There was a dusty palm in a tarnished brass bowl by the door. Five bamboo cane chairs stood around, looking as if they had never been sat in. An atmosphere of squalor brooded over the dismal scene.

I paused and looked around.

There was a shabbily dressed woman sitting in a corner in the only leather lounging chair, looking across at me, cigarette dropping from her over-made-up lips.

I didn't recognise Rima for a moment or so. Her hair was no longer silver: it was dyed a brick red and cut short in a ragamuffin style. She had on a black suit that was pretty well on its last legs. Her green shirt was grubby and had a washed-out, faded look.

I walked slowly across the lobby watched by the old negro and stood before her. We looked at each other.

The past years had been hard on her. Her face had an unhealthy pallor and was puffy. She looked older than her thirty years. The touches of rouge she had dabbed on her cheeks kidded no one except maybe herself. Her eyes were hard: the impersonal bleak eyes of a street walker: like stones dipped in blue-black ink.

It was a shock to see how she had altered. When I had heard her voice over the telephone the image of her when last I had seen her had risen up in my mind, but this woman was a stranger to me, and yet I knew it was Rima. In spite of the red hair and the hardness there was no mistaking that it was she.

I watched the stony eyes move swiftly over my suit and the

raincoat I carried on my arm and at my shoes, then they shifted to my face.

"Hello, Jeff," she said. "Long time no see."

"We'd better go somewhere where we can talk," I said, aware that my voice sounded husky.

She lifted her eyebrows.

"I wouldn't want to embarrass you. You're the big wheel now. If your rich pals saw me with you they might jump to the wrong conclusions."

"We can't talk here. Come out to the car."

She shook her head.

"We'll talk here. Don't worry about Joe. He's as deaf as a post. Are you going to buy me a drink?"

"You can have what you want."

She got up, crossed over to the reception desk and rang a bell by the negro, who shifted away from her, scowling at her.

A man came out of a back room: a big, fat Italian with greasy black hair and a heavy stubble on his chin. He was wearing a dirty cowboy shirt and a pair of dirtier flannel trousers.

"A bottle of Scotch, two glasses and charge water, Toni," Rima said, "and hurry it up."

The fat man stared at her.

"Who's paying for it?"

She nodded to me.

"He is. Hurry it up."

His black, blood-shot eyes roved over me, then he nodded and went back into the inner room.

I pulled up one of the bamboo cane chairs and arranged it so I would sit near her when she came back to her chair and yet be able to see the entrance to the lobby. I sat down.

She came back to her chair. As she walked I saw she had runs in both stockings and her shoes looked ready to fall to pieces.

"Well, it's like old times, isn't it?" she said, sitting down. "Except of course you're married now." She took out a pack of cigarettes and lit one, blowing smoke down her nostrils. "You've certainly done pretty well for yourself considering you could have spent all this time in a cell, or maybe even by now you could be fertilising the soil of a prison yard."

The fat man came with the drinks. I paid him what he asked, and after looking curiously at me, he went away and back into the inner room.

With an unsteady hand, she poured a big shot of whisky into one of the glasses, then pushed the bottle over to me.

I didn't touch it. I watched her drink half the whisky neat, then add charge water to what was left.

"You haven't much to say for yourself, have you?" she said, looking at me. "How have you been getting on all these years? Ever think of me?"

"I've thought about you," I said.

"Ever wondered what I was doing?"

I didn't say anything.

"Did you keep that tape of me singing?

Long before I had got home, I had got rid of the tape; I hadn't wanted anything to remind me of her.

"It got lost," I said woodenly.

"Did it? That's a pity. It was a good tape." She took another drink. "It was worth a whale of a lot of money. I was hoping you had kept it and I could sell it."

It was coming now. I waited.

She shrugged her shoulders.

"As you lost it, and you've made so much money, I don't suppose you'll mind paying me for it."

"I'm not paying you anything," I said.

She finished her drink and poured more whisky into her glass.

"So you're married. That's a change for you, isn't it? I thought you didn't care for women."

"We'll skip that, Rima. I don't think there's much point carrying on this conversation. You and I are in two different worlds. You had your chance. I've taken mine."

She slid her hand inside her grubby shirt to scratch her ribs. It was a gesture that brought the past back with an unpleasant impact.

"Does your wife know you murdered a man?" she asked, looking directly at me.

"I didn't murder a man," I said steadily. "And well leave my wife out of this."

"Well, okay, if you're so sure you didn't, then you won't mind if I go to the cops and tell them you did."

"Look, Rima," I said,"you know as well as I do, you shot the guard. No one would take your word against mine now. So let's skip it."

"When I saw your photo in Life, in that fine office, I couldn't believe my luck," she said. "I just managed to get here in time to catch your TV performance. So you're going to pick up sixty thousand dollars. That's a whale of a lot of money. How much are you going to give me?"

"Not a dime" I said. "Is that plain enough?"

She laughed.

"Oh, but you are. You are going to compensate me for losing that tape. I reckon it is worth sixty thousand. It's probably worth more.

72

"You heard what I said, Rima. If you try to blackmail me, I'll hand you over to the police."

She finished her drink and sat, nursing her glass, as her stony eyes moved over my face.

"I've kept the gun, Jeff," she said. "The L.A. cops have a description of you on their files. They know the man they want for murder has a drooping right eyelid and a scar along the side of his jaw. All I have to do is to walk into the nearest Station house and tell them you and I are the ones they are looking for. When I give them the gun, you'll find yourself in the death row. It's as easy and as simple as that."

"Not quite," I said. "You would be an accessory to murder even if they did believe your story against mine. You would also go to jail. Don't forget that!"

She leaned back and laughed. It was a harsh, horrible sound.

"You poor sap! Do you imagine I would care if I went to jail? Take a look at me! What have I got to lose? I'm washed-up! I've lost what looks I ever had. I can't sing a note now. I'm a junky, always on the hunt for some money to buy a shot. Why should I care if I went to jail? I'd be better off than I am now! " She leaned forward, her face suddenly changing to a vicious harshness,"But you'd care if you went to jail! You have everything to lose! You want to build that bridge, don't you? You want a new home, don't you? You want to go on sleeping with that nice wife of yours' don't you? You want to hang onto your position in life, don't you? You have everything. I have nothing. If you don't toe the line, Jeff, we'll go to jail together. I mean that. Don't think I'm bluffing. What's better than money? I want it and I'm going to have it. You're going to pay or we go to jail!"

I stared at her. What she had said was true. She had nothing to lose. She was at the bottom of civilised existence. I could even believe she would be better off in jail.

I had to try to frighten her, but I knew it was hopeless.

"They'd give you at least ten years. How would you like to be locked up in a cell for ten years without any dope?"

She laughed at me.

"How would you like to be locked up in a cell for twenty years without your nice wife? I couldn't care. Maybe they would cure me. How do you imagine I've been living these past years? How do you imagine I have managed to scrape up the money to buy my shots? I've been walking the streets. You think about it. You try to imagine that nice wife of yours coping with men every night. You can't scare me with the thoughts of jail, but I can scare you! Jail would be like a home to me after what I've been through! You either pay up or we go to jail!"

73

Looking at the desperate, degenerate face I knew I was caught. There was a case against me. Maybe I might beat the murder rap, but I was certain to land in jail. My fear turned to a smouldering rage. I had come so far. I was now right at the top. Until she had telephoned, my future was assured. Now I was in her trap. She had only to crack her whip and I would have to obey. I was sure she planned to bleed me white.

"Well, all right," I said. "I'll give you some money. I'll give you five thousand dollars. That's all I can spare. Think yourself damn lucky to get it."

"Oh no, Jeff. I have a score to settle with you. I haven't forgotten how you once treated me." She put her hand to her face. "No sonofabitch slaps me without paying for it. I'm dictating the terms. That tape you lost is going to cost you thousand dollars. I want ten thousand this week. Ten thousand on the first of the month and thirty thousand on the following month and ten thousand as a final payment."

I felt a rush of blood to my head, but I kept control of myself. "No!"

She laughed.

"All right: please yourself. You think it over, Jeff. I'm not bluffing. You either pay up or we go to jail That's the proposition. Please yourself."

I thought about it. I could see no way out. I was caught. I knew it wouldn't stop there. Once she had run through the sixty thousand, she would come back for more. The only escape from her continual blackmail would be if she died. I suddenly realised that if I were to live the life I wanted to live I would have to kill her.

The thought didn't shock me. I had no feeling for her. She was a depraved, degenerate animal. It would be like killing some disgusting insect.

I opened my cigarette case, took out a cigarette and lit it. My hands were rock steady.

"Looks as if you have me over a barrel" I said. "Well, all right. I'll get the ten thousand. I'll have it ready for you by tomorrow. If you will meet me outside here at this time, I'll give it to you."

She smiled at me: it was a smile that chilled my heart.

"I know what you are planning, Jeff. I've thought this thing out. 'I've had plenty of time to think while you have been so busy making money. I put myself in your place. How would I react, I asked myself, if I were you and found myself in such a fix?" She let smoke drift out of her open mouth as she paused, then she went on,"First, I would try to find a way out. It wouldn't take me very long to realise there is no way out except one way." She leaned forward and stared at me. "The same idea has occurred to you, hasn't it? The only way out is for me to be dead, and you're already planning to kill me, aren't you?"

I sat motionless, staring at her. The blood drained out of my face and my body felt damp and cold.

"I've taken care of that angle," she went on, and opened her shabby handbag. She took out a scrap of paper and flicked it into my lap. "You'll mail the cheques to this address. It's the address of the Pacific and Union Bank of Los Angeles. It's not my bank, but they have been told to credit my account some where else and you won't know where it is. I'm taking no chances with you. There'll be no way for you to find out where my bank is or where I'll be living. So don't imagine you are going to murder me, Jeff, because you'll never find me after tonight."

I kept control of the urge that made me want to fasten my hands around her throat and choke the life out of her.

"You seem to have thought of everything, haven't you?" I said.

"I think I have." She held out her hand. "Give me your wallet. I want some money right now."

"You can go to hell," I said.

She smiled at me.

"Remember years ago when you asked me for my purse and you took every dollar I had? Give me your wallet, Jeff, or we'll take a walk to the Station house."

We stared at each other for a long moment, then I took out my wallet and dropped it into her lap.

That morning I had been to the bank. I had two hundred dollars in the wallet. She took the lot and then tossed the wallet onto the table.

She got up, putting the money in her bag and she crossed the lobby to the reception desk and rang the bell.

The fat Italian came out of the inner room. She spoke to him. I couldn't hear what she was saying. She gave him some money. He grinned at her, nodding, then went back into the inner room.

She came back to me.

"I'm leaving now. You won't see me again unless you try something smart. You will send a cheque sometimes this week for the ten thousand dollars to the Los Angeles bank. On the first of the month you will send another cheque for ten thousand. The following month you will send me a cheque for thirty thousand. The month after that, another cheque for ten thousand. Have you got that?"

"Yes," I said, thinking if she was leaving now I must follow her. I was sure if I lost her now, I would never find her again. "But don't imagine it's going to be all that easy."

"Isn't it?"

The fat Italian, followed by two hard looking characters, came out

75

of the inner room and grouped themselves in front of the entrance to the hotel.

I was on my feet now.

"I've asked these boys to keep you here until I drop out of sight," Rima said. "I wouldn't start anything with them. They're tough."

The two men with the fat Italian were both young and strong looking. One of them, with a lot of blond limp hair, wore a leather jacket and had leather patches on the knees of his trousers. The other, with a brutal hammered face of an ex-boxer, was in a filthy white shirt, the sleeves rolled up and a pair of jeans.

"So long," Rima said to me. "Don't forget our little arrangement or we'll be meeting again in a place you won't like."

She picked up a battered suitcase that was standing, out of sight, behind her chair and walked across the lobby.

I remained motionless.

The three men stared at me, also motionless.

Rima went out of the hotel, and I saw her walk briskly down the steps and away into the darkness.

After a moment or so, the blond tough said,"Should we rough this mug up a little, Battler? Work him over a little?"

The other snorted through his broken nose.

"Why not? I ain't had any exercise for weeks."

The fat Italian said sharply, "None of that stuff. He stays here for five minutes, then he goes. No one touches him."

The blond tough spat on the floor.

"You're the boss."

We all stood there while the minutes ticked away. After what seemed a lot longer than five minutes, the fat Italian said,"Come on. Let's get back to the game."

The three of them slouched back into the inner room, leaving me alone with the old negro.

He stared at me, rubbing the back of his head with a large, black hand.

"I guess you're leading a charmed life, mister," he said. "Those guys are mean."

I went out into the night and got into my car.

II

As I drove across the City towards my home, my mind was active.

There seemed no way out of this trap. It would be impossible to find Rima again now. She could continue to blackmail me in safety and out of my reach. I would have to give her all the money I would earn from the bridge job and then more. I knew she would continue to blackmail me for the rest of her days.

I realised that Terrell's cottage was now just a pipe dream. How was I going to explain this to Sarita?

It was the thought of Sarita that stiffened my back bone. I slowed the car and pulled up at the kerb.

I couldn't take this lying down, I told myself, and a hot wave of rage ran through me. I must find a way out.

For several minutes I sat staring through the windshield at the mass of traffic moving ahead of me, trying to calm my jumping nerves. Finally, I did get control of myself and I was able to think more coolly.

Rima had given me the address of a Los Angeles bank. Did this mean that she was leaving Holland City for Los Angeles or was it just a trick to throw me off her trail?

I had to find her again. It was my only hope of survival. I had to find her and then silence her.

I started the car moving and drove fast to the Ritz-Plaza hotel, a couple of blocks ahead. Leaving the car outside, I went in and made my way to the Travel Bureau.

The girl in charge smiled brightly at me.

"Yes, sir?"

"Is there a 'plane out to Los Angeles tonight?"

"Not now, sir. The first plane out would be ten twenty-five tomorrow morning".

"How about a train?"

She picked up a time-table, flicked through the pages, then nodded.

"There's a train at eleven forty. If you hurry, you could catch it."

I thanked her and went back to my car.

I drove fast to the railroad station, parked and walked to the Information Bureau. The time was now half past eleven. They told me the Los Angeles train was due in at Platform 3.

Moving cautiously, and looking out for Rima, I went to Platform 3. I stopped by the news-stand near the entrance to the platform. The gates were still closed. There was a group of people waiting. There was no sign of Rima. I waited, keeping out of sight until the gates were opened. After a ten-minute wait I watched the train pull out. I was sure Rima wasn't on board.

I walked back to my car. It had been a shot in the dark, and it hadn't come off. Tomorrow would be hopeless. I couldn't cover both the airport and the railroad station. Anyway, it was more possible that she had given me the Los Angeles bank address to throw me off her trail. She could be planning to settle anywhere. My cheque would go to the Los Angeles bank, and they would send it on to any town in the country. It seemed an impossible task to find her.

I got in my car and drove home. As I walked from the elevator to my apartment I glanced at my wrist watch. The time was five minutes after midnight. With any luck, Sarita would be in bed. I was in such a depressed, angry mood I didn't want to talk to her tonight.

But my luck was out, as I opened the front door I saw the light was on in the lounge.

"Jeff?"

Sarita came to the door as I took off my raincoat.

"Hello, darling," I said. "I thought you would be in bed."

"I've been waiting up for you. I thought you would never come." The note in her voice made me look sharply at her. I could see she was excited about something. "Do you want anything to eat?"

Although I had had no dinner, the thought of food sickened me.

"I've had all I want, thanks. What's the excitement about?"

She linked her arm in mine and drew me into the lounge.

"Mr. Terrell telephoned a couple of hours ago. He wants an immediate decision. He has had an offer for the cottage. It's ten thousand more than he asked us. He's so kind. He said he would like us to have it and he is offering it to us at the original price, but we must let him know right away."

I moved from her and sat down.

Well, here it was. I was in it up to my neck before I had time to recover from the first body blow.

"He said he would give me a week", I said, taking out my cigarette case and lighting a cigarette.

"Yes, darling, I know he did, but this offer has just come in," Sarita said, sitting opposite me. "We can't expect him to lose ten thousand just for a couple of days. Anyway, why should we keep him waiting? We're going to have the place, aren't we? There's nothing else anything like as good, and it really is a bargain."

"Well, no," I said, not looking at her. "I don't think I'm going ahead with it, Sarita. I've been thinking it over. A home is a pretty permanent thing. I am going to spend my life in this City. Terrell's place is nice, of course, but I think the best thing to do is to hang on here for a year or so and then build a place. By then, I shall know for certain what my financial position will be. With any luck, we should be pretty well off. We might even be able to plan something a lot nicer than the bungalow. It's better to build. As soon as I've fixed the bridge, I'll get out a plan. We can work at it together. We'll have absolutely what we want."

I saw her stiffen and I could see her disappointment.

"But, Jeff dear, at this price the bungalow is a bargain. Instead of remaining in this dreary apartment for another year, we can move into the cottage, take our time about building, and when the place has been built, we can sell the cottage at a profit."

"I see that," I said, trying to control my jumping nerves. "But I'd rather wait. I think we'll forget about the cottage."

"Please, Jeff." It hurt me and made me mad to see how upset she was. "I love the place. Please change your mind. If we buy, we don't pay rent. We will save that. It's investing your money sensibly, and I really don't want to stay here another year."

"I'm sorry," I said,"but I'm not buying Terrell's place. Let's skip it, shall we? I'm tired, and I'm ready for bed."

"But, Jeff, you can't just dismiss it like that. It's important to both of us. We have the money. You agreed it was just what we want. We can't go on living here. You'll have to entertain more. We can't have people here. A man in your position must have a nice home."

"Let's skip it, Sarita. I know what I'm doing."

For a long moment she stared at me, then she said,"Well, of course, if that's the way you feel ... all right. You really want us to remain here?"

"Until we build."

"Then perhaps we could refurnish the place: at least let us try to make it look something better than this."

"We'll talk about that later." I got to my feet. "Let's go to bed. Look at the time: it's pushing one o'clock."

"Mr. Terrell is waiting, Jeff. He wants to know tonight."

This was more than my nerves could take.

"Well, tell him then! Tell him I've changed my mind," and I went out of the lounge and into the bedroom.

I was angry and sick with frustration. As I began to undress, I heard Sarita talking on the telephone.

I was under the shower when she came into the bedroom. After I had put on my pyjamas, I joined her in the bedroom. I got into bed and lit a cigarette.

She went into the bathroom and shut the door. This was the first time since we had married that she had shut the door while preparing for bed and its significance wasn't lost on me.

I suddenly had to know the exact amount of money I had in the bank. I got out of bed, went into the lounge and got out my bank statement. A quick calculation showed that I had a little less than two thousand dollars in cash and ten thousand in bonds. I wouldn't be getting my share of the bridge fee for another eight days.

We had been spending my small capital pretty briskly since I had landed the bridge contract. There had been clothes to buy. I had given Sarita a diamond brooch. I had had new tyres fitted to the car.

I would have to part with my bonds to Rima. That left me with two thousand for eight days, plus a lot of bills.

I returned to the bedroom.

Sarita was already in bed, her back to my bed.

I got into bed and turned off the light.

"Good night darling," I said.

"Good night."

Her voice was flat and impersonal.

"I'm sorry, Sarita. Really sorry, but you must believe I know what I'm doing," I said. "You won't regret it in the long run. Try not to be too disappointed."

"I don't want to discuss it any more. Good night."

There was silence,

I lay there staring into the darkness, feeling pretty bad. After a while I switched my mind to what I was going to do. If I were to save our future, I had to find a way out of this mess.

There were three obvious things I had to do: find Rima, find the gun and get rid of it, then silence Rima.

But how was I going to find her?

Tomorrow I would have to send a cheque for ten thousand dollars to the Los Angeles bank. As far as I could see, the only possible way to trace Rima was through this bank. Obviously, they wouldn't give me her address, but was it possible to trick it out of them in some way?

I thought about this for some time, but finally decided it was a hopeless line of thought. Somewhere in the bank they would have a record of Rima's other bank and her signed instructions to credit any sum paid to them into this bank. Was it possible for me to get at this record?

How did one get at the records held by a bank, short of break in at night? That would be completely beyond my powers. To break into a bank was a professional job, and besides, the risk of being caught was almost a sure thing.

After more thought, I decided it was impossible to make any plan until I had seen the bank. This meant a trip to Los Angeles.

I thought of all the work piled up on my desk and the appointments I had lined up for tomorrow and I cursed Rima. But my work would have to be shelved. If I was going to find her I would have to act at once.

I would have to take the ten-thirty plane tomorrow morning. Jack would have to handle the urgent appointments. What he would say I couldn't imagine, but I had to move fast. There was a slight chance that Rima would be going to Los Angeles and a slighter chance that I might spot her.

I would have to part with the first ten thousand dollars. I then had three clear weeks ahead of me before I had to pay the second instalment. In that time I had to find and silence her.

CHAPTER THREE

I

I GOT to the office before eight o'clock and I was in a pretty depressed mood.

Sarita had been quiet during breakfast. We had said little to each other. Nothing was said about the bungalow, but it was there, between us like a ten-foot wall.

When I looked at my desk and saw all the paper work piled in my In-tray, my heart sank. By going to Los Angeles, I would be throwing a hopeless burden on Jack. I knew he was pretty booked up this morning with appointments with contractors at the site of the bridge.

I slaved for an hour, getting some of the urgent paper work out of the way, then the door jerked open and Jack breezed in.

"Hi, Jeff!" he said, going over to his desk. "I've got four bull dozers on the job. They are beginning to clear the site right now. I've started them, now I've got to see Cooper about those concrete mixers. Any mail in yet?"

"Not yet." I hesitated, then blurted out, "Look, Jack, I've got to take a couple of days off."

He was pawing through a mass of papers, muttering under his breath. For a moment, he didn't seem to have heard, then he looked up sharply.

"What was that?"

I leaned back in my desk chair and tried to look casual.

"I have to take a couple of days off. I want you to hold the fort."

He stared at me as if he thought I had gone crazy.

"Hey! Wait a minute! You can't do that! You can't take time off now, Jeff! What are you thinking of! You have Kobey, Max Stone, Crombie and Cousins lined up for appointments, haven't you? I want those estimates for the steel today. You can't take time off now!"

"I'm sorry, but I have to. This is very urgent private business."

His jovial face suddenly turned hard and flushed brick red.

"I don't give a damn how urgent it is! We're building a bridge and we have a time limit! To hell with your urgent and private business! You've got to stay right here and do your job as I'm doing mine!"

"But I have to go, Jack."

He ran his hand over his balding head, staring at me. Slowly, the flush died down and into his alert eyes came a quizzmg, shrewd expression.

"What's up then?"

"Personal trouble," I said woodenly, not looking at him. "It's important to Sarita and me."

He moved papers about on his desk, frowning, then he said, "I'm sorry I blew up. I'm sorry too to hear you have trouble. Let's put our cards on the table, Jeff. You and I are partners. We have put our money in this firm and we're in it together. We have landed the biggest job the City can offer us. If we fall down on it, were cooked. Make no mistake about that. I don't know what your trouble is, but I'm reminding you this job represents my future as well as yours. If you miss these appointments, we'll lose five working days. There's no two ways about that. If Mathison takes it into his head to telephone and finds you're not at your desk, he'll hit the ceiling. I'm making an issue of this, Jeff, because neither of us can nor should take a minute off for at least two months." He lifted his shoulders in a shrug. "Well, I've said my piece. It's up to you what you do. If you take time off now, the bridge will be five days late, and we will have fallen down on the job, and we won't get any more jobs like this one. I know it, and nothing you say will alter the facts."

I knew he was right. I felt a murderous impulse go through me as I realised that Rima must have counted on this, had counted on me being chained to Holland City so she could hide herself away in her own time and with the confidence that once she was hidden, I could never find her.

I hesitated for a long moment, then I gave up. I had to think of Jack and the bridge even if it meant sacrificing myself. I would have to wait. It would make the hunt for Rima much more difficult and I stood to lose my second ten thousand dollars, but I had no alternative.

"Okay, forget it," I said. "I'm sorry to have brought it up."

"Sorry-hell! You've got to stay here, Jeff, or we'll be sunk! Now we have that little item off our chests, what's the trouble? You and I are partners. I'm not that stupid I can't see by looking at you that there is something badly wrong. It's a good thing to share bad things: share this with me."

I very nearly told him, but I stopped in time.

My only way out of this mess was to find and silence Rima. I couldn't bring Jack into it. This was something I had to do on my own. I would be making him an accessory to murder.

"It's something I have to handle myself," I said, looking away from him. "Thanks all the same."

"That's up to you," he said and I could see he was hurt and worried. "I won't press it. I want to put on record that if you want help, financial or otherwise, I'm here. I'm your partner. What concerns you, concerns me. Understand?"

"Thanks, Jack."

We looked at each other, slightly embarrassed, then he got to his feet and began collecting his papers.

"Well, I've got to get going. I have a couple of guys waiting for me right now."

When he had gone, I took out my cheque book and wrote a cheque for ten thousand dollars in favour of Rima Marshall. I put the cheque in an envelope, addressed it to the Los Angeles bank and put it in my Out-tray. Then I 'phoned my bank and told them to sell my bonds.

I was caught, but I was still determined to find Rima if I could before I parted with any more money. If I really got down to the job and worked practically non-stop, I could gain a few days breathing space. I had three weeks in which to clear my desk, and to get so far ahead with my work I could afford a few days off: three weeks before the second payment was due.

I went to work.

I doubt if any man at any time has ever slaved harder than I did during the next two weeks. I worked like a crazy man.

I was at my desk at half-past five in the morning and I worked through until past midnight. During those two weeks, I scarcely said more than a dozen words to Sarita. I left her asleep, and on my return found her in bed. I drove my contractors nearly out of their minds. I turned poor Clara into a thin, sunken-eyed automaton. I got so far ahead with my work that Jack couldn't keep pace with me.

"For the love of mike!" he exploded after the twelfth day, "we're not finishing this goddam bridge next week! Ease off, will you? My boys are going nuts under this pressure!"

"Let them go nuts!" I said. "I have everything buttoned up on my side, and I'm taking three days off from tomorrow. By the time I get back, you should have caught up. Have you any complaints if I take three days off?"

Jack lifted his hands in a gesture of surrender.

"I'd welcome it! Seriously, Jeff, I've never seen anyone work the way you have worked these last two weeks. You have earned your days off. Okay, go wherever you want to, but there is just one thing: if you are in as bad a spot as I think you must be, I want to share it with you."

"I can handle it," I said. "Thanks all the same."

I got home around eleven o'clock: the first time I had been

reasonably early for two weeks. Sarita was preparing for bed as I walked into the apartment.

She had got over her disappointment about the cottage by now, and we were more or less on the usual terms: perhaps not quite, but close enough. I knew she had been watching the way I had been working, and it had been worrying her.

I was feeling pretty knocked out, but knowing that at last I was going on the hunt for Rima kept me going.

"I'm leaving for New York tomorrow first thing," I said. "There are a number of things I have to take care of, and I'll be away for three or four days. I've got to get a lower estimate for a bunch of items to do with the bridge, and New York is the only place where I'll get what I want."

She came to me and put her arms around me.

"You're killing yourself, Jeff. Surely you don't have to work this hard?"

She looked up at me, her brown eyes worried.

"It'll ease off. It's been tough, but I had to clear my desk before I could make this trip."

"Darling, could I go with you? I haven't been to New York for years. I'd love it. We could meet after your business dates, and while you are tied up, I could look around the shops."

Why I hadn't thought that she would want to come with me I can't imagine. It was the most obvious thing she would suggest. For a long, painful moment I stared at her, not able to think up an excuse to put her off. Maybe I said all I need to have said by looking at her like this. I saw the excitement die out of her eyes and her face fell.

"I'm sorry," she said and turned away and began to straighten the cushions on the settee. "Of course you won't want me around. I wasn't thinking. I'm sorry I mentioned it."

I drew in a long slow breath. I hated seeing her look like this. I hated to hurt her as I knew I had hurt her.

"It just so happens, Sarita, I will be tied up morning, noon and night. I'm sorry, too, but I think it would be better if you stayed here this trip. Next trip will be different."

"Yes." She moved across the room. "Well, I guess we had better go to bed."

It wasn't until I had turned off the light and we were isolated in our twin beds that she said out of the darkness,"Jeff, what are we going to do with our money? Anything?"

If I didn't find her and kill her, we were going to give our money to Rima, but I didn't tell Sarita this.

"We're going to build a place of our own," I said, but there was no confidence in my voice. "We're going to have some fun as soon as I get all this work behind me."

"Jack has bought a Thunderbird," Sarita said. "He has paid out twelve thousand dollars to redecorate and furnish his apartment. What have we done with our share of the money?"

"Never mind about Jack. He's a bachelor and he doesn't have to worry about his future. I've got to be sure you are taken care of if anything happened to me."

"Does that mean I shall have to wait until you are dead or we are old before spending a dime of it?"

"Now, look . . ." The irritation in my voice sounded harsh even to me. "We'll spend the money . . ."

"I'm sorry. I was only asking. It seems odd that you should make sixty thousand dollars, and yet we still live the same way, still wear the same clothes, never go anywhere, never do anything, and I can't even go to New York with you. I suppose I'm being unreasonable, but for the life of me I can't see why you are working like a slave day in and night out and neither of us are having any fun out of it."

I felt a hot rush of blood to my head. Goaded beyond endurance, I lost control of my temper.

"For Heaven's sake, Sarita," I yelled at her. "Stop this! I'm trying to build a bridge! I haven't even got the money yet! We'll spend it when I've got it!"

There was a pause, then she said in a cold, shocked voice, "I'm sorry. I didn't mean to irritate you."

Then followed a deadly silence. It went on and on. We both knew the other was awake, unable to sleep, worried and bitterly hurt.

The shadowy ghost of Rima stood between our beds, pushing us apart, threatening our happiness.

I had to find her.

I had to rid myself of her.

II

I arrived at Los Angeles Airport a little after one o'clock and took a taxi to the Pacific and Union Bank.

Every spare moment, and they were few, that I had had during the past two weeks, I had wracked my brains as to how I was to get the address of Rima's other bank. It was certain the Pacific and Union would have a record of the address, and my first move was to try to find out how and where this record was kept.

As I paid off the taxi, I was relieved to see that the bank was a big one. I had feared it might have been a small branch affair with only a few staff who would remember me. But this was a vast building with a commissionaire on the door, and a continuous flow of customers going in and out.

I walked into the big reception hall. On either side were the grills behind which stood the tellers. At every station was a small group of people, waiting. Around and behind these stations was a gallery where I could see clerks busy with calculating machines, duplicators and such like. At the far end of the hall I could see the glass cages for the bank officers.

I walked to one of the grills and got behind the short queue. Murmuring apologies, I reached over and took a pay-in slip from the rack. From my wallet I took ten five dollar bills. After a few minutes, there was only one customer ahead of me and I could reach the counter. I wrote in bold block letters at the head of the pay-in slip *Rita Marschal,* and at the foot of the slip, I wrote: paid in by *John Hamilton.*

The man in front of me moved away and I pushed the ten five dollar bills and the pay-in slip under the grill.

The teller took the slip, lifted his rubber stamp, then paused and frowned. He glanced up at me.

I was leaning against the counter, staring away from him, my face expressionless.

"I don't think this is correct, sir," he said to me.

I turned and stared at him.

"What do you mean?"

He hesitated, looked again at the pay-in slip, then said,"If you will wait a moment..."

It was working out the way I had hoped it would. He took the slip and leaving his station, he walked briskly down the long counter to the stairs that led up to the gallery. I stood back so I could watch him. He went up the stairs and along the gallery to where a girl was sitting at a big machine. He spoke to her. She swung around in her chair to a big card that hung on the wall. I watched her run her finger down what seemed a list of names, then she turned to the machine, pressed buttons, and after a moment, she reached forward and then gave the teller a card.

My heart was thumping.

I knew then that she had operated an automatic Finding and Filing machine which could produce the card containing particulars of any client by pressing numbered keys: each client having his or her own particular number.

When the keys were pressed, the card would be shot into a tray.

I watched the teller study the card and then my pay-in slip. He gave the card to the girl and then hurried back to me.

"There is some mistake here, sir," he said"We have no account in this name. Are you sure you have the name right?"

I shrugged my shoulders impatiently.

"I wouldn't swear to it. This happens to be a bridge debt. I was playing against Miss Marschal and I lost. I hadn't my cheque book with me. I promised to pay what I owe her into this bank. I understand she doesn't bank here, but you look after any money paid in."

He stared at me.

"That is right, sir, if it's the client we deal with, but her name isn't Marschal. It wouldn't be Rima Marshall. The name having no 'c' and two 'lls'?"

"I wouldn't know," I said. "Maybe I had better check." Then very casually, I went on, "I don't happen to have her address. Maybe you can give it to me?"

He took that without a blink.

"If you will address your letter care of the bank, sir, we'll be happy to forward it."

I was pretty sure he would say exactly that, but all the same, I was disappointed.

"I'll do that. Thanks."

"You're welcome, sir."

I nodded to him, put the money back in my wallet and walked out.

That was the first move. I now knew where the record card was kept. I now had to get at it.

I took a taxi to a quiet, inexpensive hotel, booked in, and as soon as I got to my room, I telephoned the Pacific and Union bank. I asked to be put through to the manager.

When he came on the line, I introduced myself as Edward Masters and asked him if he could see me around ten o'clock the following morning. I said there was some business I wanted to discuss with him.

He made an appointment for ten fifteen.

It irked me that I could do nothing further until the following morning, but this was something I couldn't rush. I was acutely aware that thirteen years ago the Los Angeles police had been searching for a man with a drooping eyelid and a scar on his jaw. For all I knew there might be some keen veteran who might recognise me even now so I spent the rest of the day in the hotel lounge, and I went to bed early.

The following morning I arrived at the bank at a minute to quarter past ten.

I was shown immediately into the manager's office.

The manager, a fat, elderly man with a bedside manner, shook my hand heartily. At the same time he managed to convey that he was pretty busy and it would be all right with him if I got down to business without wasting too much of his time.

I told him I was representing a firm of building contractors. I said we had our head office in New York and we were planning to set up a branch office in Los Angeles. We had decided to bank with Pacific and Union, and I gave him to understand we were pretty big operators. I asked his advice about obtaining premises. I said we would need plenty of room as we had ten executives and a staff of over two hundred. I could see that made an impression on him. He gave me the name of an Estate Agent who, he told me, could fix me up. I told him we planned to transfer about two million dollars from our New York bank to his to give us a start. That impressed him too.

Anything he could do, he told me, he would be pleased to do. I had only to ask and the services of the bank would be at my disposal.

"I don't think there is," I said. Then after a pause I went on, "Maybe there is one thing. I see you have a pretty up-to-date office equipment system here. This is something I want to install in our offices. Who are the people to go to?"

"Chandler and Carrington are the best people," he said. "They have all the necessary equipment you would need."

"In a way, our business is a little like yours," I said, moving cautiously to the reason why I was sitting facing him. "We have clients all over. We need to keep in touch with them. We need records of our association with them. There's a file and finding machine you have here. I'm interested in it. Do you find it satisfactory?"

I was lucky. It seemed this particular machine was something in which he took a lot of pride.

"It has proved more than satisfactory. I admit it is expensive, but in the long run, it can't be beaten."

"I only caught a glimpse of it as I came in," I said. "You really are pleased with it?"

"Look, Mr. Masters, if you're interested, I'd be happy for you to see a demonstration. We are more than satisfied. Would you care to see the machine operating?"

I forced myself to sound casual.

"I don't want to bother you...."

"It's no bother: it's a pleasure." He pressed a button on his desk. "I'll get Mr. Flemming to show it to you."

"As soon as we find the right premises, I'll be in touch with you again," I said. "I appreciate your help."

88

A clerk appeared in the doorway: an earnest looking guy who waited hopefully and expectantly.

"Flemming, this is Mr. Masters' He will be opening an account with us. Mr. Masters is interested in our Filing and Finding machine. Will you demonstrate it to him?"

"Yes, sir." The guy bowed to me. "It'll be a pleasure."

I got up. My legs felt shaky. I knew I was half way there, but half way there wasn't enough. I shook hands with the manager, again thanked him for his help, then followed Flemming out of the office, up the stairs and along the gallery.

We stopped by the machine.

A girl, sitting before it, swung her chair around and looked at us inquiringly.

Flemming introduced me, then he went ahead and explained how the machine worked.

"We have three thousand five hundred odd clients," he told me. "Each client has a number. We keep a list of numbers right here on this card."

He pointed to a big card hanging on the wall. I walked over to it and stared at it, my eyes moving over it swiftly. I found Rima's name. It looked odd to me to see the neat lettering that spelt out: *Rima Marshall. 2997.*

My mind absorbed the number: it absorbed it the way I have never absorbed any other thing before in my life.

"Having got the number," Flemming went on,"all we have to do is to press the keys that make up the number and the record card is immediately dropped into the tray here."

"That sounds fine," I said, smiling at him,"but does it work?" The girl who had been listening gave me a pitying smile.

"It never fails."

"Give me a demonstration," I said, smiling back at her.

"Take the first number on our list," Flemming said. "R. Aitken. His number is 0001. Miss Laker, give me Mr. Aitken's card."

She swung around, pressed the keys. The machine hummed into life and a card fell into a tray.

"Just like that," Flemming said, beaming at me.

I held out my hand.

"I'm a sceptic. Maybe the card has nothing to do with Mr. Aitken."

Happily, he handed the card to me.

I saw it had Aitken printed in large type at the top of the card.

"Yes. It's impressive. Looks like I'll have to invest in a machine like this. Could I have a try?"

"Certainly, Mr. Masters. You go ahead."

I bent over the keyboard. I pressed down the keys that spelt out 2997.

My heart was thumping so violently I was scared he and the girl would hear it.

The machine hummed. The cards flicked through the metal holder. I stood there, feeling sweat on my face, watching and waiting, then I saw the lone white card slide into the tray.

Flemming and the girl smiled.

"The number you selected belongs to Miss Rima Marshall," Flemming said. "See for yourself if it is the correct card."

I reached out and picked up the card.

There it was:

Rima Marshall. Account. *Santa Barba. credit $10,000.*

"Some machine," I said, trying to keep my voice steady. "Well, thanks. This is just what I'm looking for."

Half an hour later, in a hired car, I was driving fast along the coast road to Santa Barba.

I told myself not to be too optimistic. Although I had narrowed down the field, although I was pretty sure Rima must be living somewhere in the locality of Santa Barba, I had still to find her and my time was running out.

I arrived in Santa Barba around five thirty. I asked a traffic cop where I could find the Pacific and Union Bank and he directed me.

I cruised past the bank which was closed. It was a branch bank and small. I parked the car and walked back to take a close look at it.

Exactly opposite was a small hotel.

I took my bag from the car and went over to the hotel. It was one of those down-at-the-heel places that cater mainly for travelling salesmen.

The fat woman behind the reception desk handed me a pen to sign in and gave me a dismal smile of welcome.

I asked her if she had a room overlooking the street. She said she had, although she recommended the back rooms as they were less noisy.

I said I didn't mind the noise, so she gave me a key and told me how to reach the room. She said dinner would be served at seven o'clock.

I carried my bag up the stairs, found the room, unlocked the door and entered.

It was clean, plain and far from comfortable, but I didn't care. I crossed to the window and looked out. Exactly opposite was the bank.

I pulled up a chair and sat down by the window and studied the grill guarding the entrance.

When did Rima visit the bank?

I knew I dare not try the same trick I had worked on the Los Angeles branch to get a look at her record card. I knew if she got the slightest hint that I was on her trail, she would slip away, and I would have to start the taunt all over again.

Maybe if I sat at this window and watched, I might see her, and then I could follow her and find out where she lived.

I realised this would take time. I was due back at my desk the day after tomorrow. I couldn't stay away longer than another day. Maybe I would have some luck and spot her. It was something I decided to do, although I didn't have much hope that tomorrow she would come to the bank.

I had to be careful to keep off the streets. It would be fatal to my plans if she saw me before I saw her. So I decided to take no chances and remain in the hotel and keep out of sight.

I unpacked, took a shower, changed, then went down to the lobby. The place was deserted. I spent some minutes checking the telephone directory and a street directory on the off chance that Rima would be listed in either one or the other, but she wasn't.

Then I went up to my room and stretched out on the bed. There was nothing now I could do until the bank opened the following morning.

The hours crawled by.

Later, I went down to the restaurant and had a cheerless dinner, badly cooked and indifferently served.

After dinner I went up to my room and went to bed.

At breakfast the following morning, I told the fat woman I had a lot of paper work to do and I planned to work in my bed-room.

She said I wouldn't be disturbed.

I returned to my room, pulled up a chair and sat down at the window.

The bank opened at nine o'clock. It was obvious that it wasn't a busy branch. For the first two hours only five people entered. After that it got a little busier, but not much. I sat there and watched.

I didn't give up hope until the bank doors were shut, then I became so depressed I could have cut my throat.

I had to leave the next morning, and I knew my chance of finding Rima before the second payment came due was now washed out.

I spent the rest of the evening, trying to think of any other way of finding her except this hit and miss chance of watching the bank, but I just couldn't think of any other way.

It would be hopeless to walk the streets in the hope of seeing her.

Besides, it would be dangerous. She could easily see me before I saw her, and then she would vanish.

Then I had a sudden idea. How would it be, I asked myself, if I employed a detective agency to find her for me?

For a few moments I was so excited by this idea I nearly rushed downstairs to consult the classified directory to find out the name and address of an agency, but then I realised I didn't dare do it.

When I found her, *I was going to kill her.*

The detective agency would remember me. They would tell the police that I had hired them to look for her, and the police would start hunting for me.

This thing was between Rima and myself. No one could help me. I had to handle it myself.

It was then, as I lay on the bed, that I realised, that even when I did find her, I still had to think of a way of killing her in complete safety.

I didn't flinch from the thought of killing her. It was Sarita's and my future against Rima's worthless and degenerate life. But it would have to be done so that it could never be traced back to me.

Had she confided in anyone that she was blackmailing me? Again that was something I had to find out. The whole thing now took on a nightmarish atmosphere: one difficulty led to another that led to another.

First, I had to find her.

Then I would have to be guided by circumstances as to how best to kill her.

Then I had to be quite, quite sure the murder couldn't be traced to me.

The following morning I took the plane to Holland City and walked into my office soon after eleven o'clock.

Jack was talking on the telephone. When he saw me, he said, "I'll call you back. Yeah. In ten minutes'. Something has come up.. ." and he dropped the receiver onto its cradle.

He looked at me and I saw at once that something bad had happened. He was pale; there were shadows under his eyes as if he hadn't had any sleep, and an expression on his usually cheerful face that sent a chill crawling up my spine.

"Have you been home yet, Jeff?"

"No. I'm just off a plane."

I put down my suitcase and dropped my raincoat on a chair.

"I've been trying to get you," Jack said, his voice husky and unsteady. "Where the hell have you been?"

"What's up?"

He hesitated, then got slowly to his feet.

"It's Sarita ..."

I felt my heart miss a beat, then it began to thump violently.

"What is it?"

"It's bad, Jeff. There's been an accident ... I tried everywhere I could think of to find you...."

I was cold and shaking now.

"She's not dead?"

"No, but she's pretty badly hurt. Some drunken driver hit her car. I'm afraid she is really badly hurt, Jeff."

I stood there, staring at him, feeling empty and cold and very lonely.

"When did it happen?"

"The morning you left. She went shopping. This drunk was on his wrong side

"Jack! Tell me! How bad is she?"

He came around the desk and put his hand on my arm.

"They are doing their best. It's a matter of waiting. You can't see her. No one can see her. As soon as there's news, they'll telephone here. She stands a chance, but it's a small one."

"Where is she?"

"The State Hospital. But look ....."

I ran out, past the white-faced Clara and down the corridor to the elevator. Somehow I got down onto the street and waved frantically to a taxi.

"State Hospital," I said, jerking open the door,"and hurry!

The driver took one look at my face, then he slammed the door shut, engaged gear and sent the cab racing down the side streets, missing the traffic while I sat rigid, my hands clenched on my knees.

I kept thinking that while I was hunting for Rima, the one person who meant everything in the world to me had been lying in a hospital bed. My hatred for Rima became a cold and deadly thing.

It took ten minutes of fast, reckless driving to get me to the hospital.

As I paid the driver, he said, "Your wife?"

"Yes."

I started up the steps, three at a time.

He shouted after me, "Good luck, bud. Good luck!"

93

CHAPTER FOUR

I

DR. WEINBORG was a tall, stoop-shouldered man with a big hooked nose, a sensitive mouth and the dark, limpid eyes of a Jew who has known suffering.

As soon as I told the nurse at the reception desk my name, she had taken me immediately to Dr. Weinborg's office. Now I was sitting, facing him and listening to his guttural voice as he said,"It's a matter of time, Mr. Halliday. I have done everything possible for your wife-anyway, for the immediate present. It was unfortunate that you were away when she was admitted. For twelve hours or so she was conscious and she was asking for you. She is now unconscious. It depends on a number of factors if she will regain consciousness. This is something I want to discuss with you. She has severe injuries to the brain. There is one good man who specialises in this kind of operation. It is dangerous and very difficult, but he has had a lot of success. I think he would give her a fifty-fifty chance. Dr. Goodyear's fee would be three thousand dollars. There would, of course, be other expenses. You would have to reckon on at least five thousand dollars, and there would be no guarantee of success."

"I don't care what it costs," I said. "Get Goodyear. Spend anything you like."

He picked up the telephone receiver and called Goodyear's residence.

It took some minutes to get a connection and some further minutes for Dr. Weinborg to convince Goodyear's receptionist of the urgency of the case. It chilled my blood to hear him explain Sarita's injuries. Half of what he said I didn't understand, but some of it I did and that told me as nothing else could how bad she was.

The receptionist said she would call him back and he hung up.

"It'll be all right, Mr. Halliday. He has never refused an urgent appeal. He'll come."

"Could I see her?"

"There's not much point. She's unconscious."

"All the same I want to see her."

He studied me, then nodded.

"Come with me."

He led me down corridors, through swing doors, up a flight of stairs to a door where a thick-set man sat on a chair, smoking.

The man, every inch a cop, looked at me without interest, but to Weinborg, he said, "As soon as she comes out of it, I want to talk to her. We can't hold this punk for ever."

94

"It'll be some time," Weinborg said, turned the door handle and opened the door.

I stood at the foot of the bed, looking down at Sarita. Her head was bandaged. The sheet was drawn up to her chin. She looked small and so white and waxy, she could have been dead.

There was a nurse sitting by the bed. She got to her feet and looked at Weinborg. She shook her head slightly at him: the secret signs between nurse and doctor.

This was the worst moment in my life. I stood there looking down at her and I had an instinctive feeling she would never speak to me again, never look at me again and never hold me in her arms again.

When I got to my apartment, and as I opened the front door, I heard the telephone bell ringing.

I picked up the receiver.

It was Mayor Mathison.

"Jeff? I've been trying to get you. Jack told me you had gone to the hospital. How is she?"

"The same. They are getting a brain specialist. There's to be an operation".

"Hilda and I keep thinking of you. Is there anything we can do?"

In a flat, toneless voice I thanked him and said there was nothing" he could do. I said it all depended now on the brain specialist.

"You'll want money, Jeff. I've already talked to the committee. They are advancing half your fee right away. You'll have thirty thousand dollars in your bank by tomorrow. We've got to save her! She's the sweetest, nicest...."

I couldn't take much more of this.

"Thank you" I said, breaking in on him and I hung up.

I began to pace up and down. I was still at it when I heard the front door bell ring.

It was Jack.

"Well? What news?"

I told him about the brain specialist.

He dropped into an armchair and rubbed his fingers across his eyes.

"You know how I feel about this. I don't have to tell you. Now listen, let's talk business for a moment. Hers, yours and my future depends on building this goddam bridge. Here's what I suggest. I've found a young guy, just out of college, who can handle your work. You've set it up and he can follow it out. You'll want to stay close to the hospital. This guy and I can cope with the office for at least a month. That will give you time to get your bearings and to be with Sarita. Okay?"

"Yes, if you're sure he can handle it."

"For a month, he can do it, but after that you'll have to take over again. By the way, Jeff, if you want any money call on me."

"Thanks," I said. "I can manage."

"Well, I just looked in." He got to his feet. "I have a whale of a lot of work to do still. Don't worry too much. She's young. You see: she'll pull out of this. Anything I can do?"

"No, thanks, Jack. I'll be here if you want me. I told them I'd be waiting here. There seemed no point in waiting at the hospital."

"That's right. Well . . ." I could see he wanted to get off. Although the important thing in my life was Sarita, the important thing in his life was the bridge. I understood, but right at that moment I didn't give a damn if the bridge was ever built. "Take it easy, Jeff." He started for the door, paused to look at me. "Did that other little trouble clear up? Anything I can do there?"

"That's under control."

He nodded and went away. I heard his heavy steps pounding on the stairs. He moved like a man in a hurry.

I lit a cigarette, but after two puffs I stubbed it out.

In eight days' time I had to pay Rima another ten thousand. Thirty days after that, I would have to pay her thirty thousand. I was sure she wouldn't stop there. She would go on and on and on, bleeding me white. With the doctors' and hospital bills ahead of me, I didn't dare part with any more money and yet I didn't dare not pay her. She was crazy enough to set the police on me, and I'd find myself in a cell when Sarita needed me most.

I paced to and fro, wondering what to do. I couldn't go to Santa Barba now Sarita was so dangerously ill, but I had to do something.

Finally, I decided to ask Rima for time to pay.

I wrote to her. I explained about Sarita's accident. I said until I knew what my expenses were, I couldn't pay out any more money to her, but later I would give her something.

I don't know why I imagined she would be merciful. Maybe I was so upset and scared, I wasn't in my right mind. If I had thought for a moment and remembered who I was writing to, I wouldn't have sent the letter, but I wasn't in the state for clear thinking.

I got the janitor to send the letter by fast night rate. She would get it the day after tomorrow if the Los Angeles bank forwarded it right away.

Around eight o'clock the hospital called and said Dr. Goodyear had arrived and would I come over right away?

Dr. Goodyear was a short, fat man with a bald head and a curt manner.

He said he intended to operate right away.

"I don't want you to be under any illusion, Mr. Halliday," he said. "Your wife is in a dangerous state. The operation is a difficult one. Frankly, the odds are against her, but I will do my best. I think you should stay here."

The next three hours were the longest and most horrible I have ever lived through. Around ten o'clock Jack came into the waiting-room and sat with me. We didn't say anything to each other. A little later Mayor Mathison and his wife came in. Mrs. Mathison touched my shoulder as she passed me, and they sat down to share the wait with me.

At twelve thirty-five, a nurse came to the door and beckoned to me.

No one said anything, but as I got to my feet and crossed the room I knew they were praying for Sarita.

In the corridor I saw Clara sitting on an upright chair, a handkerchief pressed to her eyes. Leaning against the wall, looking embarrassed, was the foreman and four of the guys who ran the bulldozers. They had come along to share my wait, and I could see how anxious they were.

I followed the nurse to Dr. Weinborg's office.

Dr. Goodyear, looking old and tired, was smoking, resting his fat hams on the edge of the desk, Dr. Weinborg stood by the window.

"Well, Mr. Halliday," Goodyear said, "the operation has been successful. Now, of course, it depends on how she rides the after effects. I think I can say she is going to live."

But there was something in the tone of his voice and in the atmosphere that warned me that this was no time for rejoicing.

"Well, go on ... what else?"

My voice sounded thick and harsh.

"The injuries to the brain are extensive," Goodyear said quietly. "Although I believe she will live, I regret to tell you she will always be an invalid." He paused, frowning, looking away from me. "I'm sure you would want the exact truth. At best she will have to live in a wheel chair. I suspect her speech may be impaired, and there seems a possibility that her memory will also be affected." He looked up then and I saw his eyes were defeated and sad. "I'm sorry. There's nothing I can say to you that can give you any comfort, but at least, I am fairly confident she will live."

I stood staring at him.

"You call that success?" I said. "She won't walk again. She'll have difficulty in talking and she won't remember me? You call that success?"

"It was a miracle that Dr. Goodyear saved her life," Dr. Weinborg said, turning from the window.

"Her life? What kind of life? Wouldn't she be better dead?"

97

I went out of the room and walked fast down the corridor. Jack was standing in the doorway of the waiting-room. He caught hold of my arm, but I pulled free and kept on.

I walked out of the hospital into the dark night and kept walking.

I had some stupid idea that if I went on and on, I could walk away from this nightmare, out of the darkness, and into the light, and then come home and find Sarita there as she had always been there since our marriage, waiting for me.

Just a stupid idea.

II

During the next three days I lived in a vacuum. I remained at home, waiting for the telephone bell to ring.

Sarita hovered between unconscious life and death.

I was alone, not wanting anyone, scarcely bothering to eat, but smoking continuously, while I sat in an armchair and waited.

From time to time Jack looked in, but he only stayed a few minutes, realising I wanted to be alone. No one telephoned, knowing that I waited for a call from the hospital and that a ring would be a knife stab if it wasn't the hospital.

Around nine o'clock on the third night of waiting the telephone did ring.

I crossed the room and snatched up the receiver.

"Yes? Halliday here."

"I want to talk to you."

It was Rima: there was no mistaking her voice. I felt my heart give a lurch, then it began to beat violently.

"Where are you?"

"In the bar of the Aster Hotel. I'm waiting. How soon can you come over?"

"Right away," I said, and hung up. I called the hospital and told the receptionist that I would be in the bar of the Aster Hotel, and if she had any news for me she would find me there.

It was raining.

I put on my raincoat, turned off the lights and went down to the street. I picked up a taxi and was driven across town to the Aster.

During the drive, a cold feeling of fear built up inside me. I was sure Rima wouldn't have come all this way to see me unless she had something in mind, and that something would be of profit to her.

The Aster Hotel was the best hotel in Holland City. Already she was changing her way of life. She was making use of my money. I felt sure she had come to extract her pound of flesh.

I wouldn't dare move beyond the reach of a telephone. She could dictate her terms and leave, and I couldn't attempt to follow her: couldn't track her down to some safe place where I could silence her. Any moment I might get a call, telling me to come at once to the hospital. I was in a trap, and no doubt she guessed it, otherwise she wouldn't have taken the risk of meeting me.

I walked into the Aster's bar. At that hour it was nearly empty. There were three men leaning against the bar, talking in under-tones and drinking Scotch. At a table in a corner, two middle-aged women were chatting over champagne cocktails. In another corner was a young, broad-shouldered, powerfully built man, wearing a cream-coloured sports coat, a red and white scarf knotted at his throat, a pair of bottle green slacks and nigger brown reverse calf shoes.

I noticed him because of his coarse, bovine handsomeness. He looked like a truck driver who has come into money. He was obviously ill at ease in the surroundings of a luxury hotel. He was holding a highball in a big, brown hand. His coarse featured face, handsome because of an animal sensuality, had a bewildered expression.

I glanced away from him, looking for Rima.

She sat in the middle of the bar, isolated by empty chairs and tables. I scarcely recognised her. She was wearing a black coat over a green dress and she had had her hair dyed the latest sable and grey style. She looked as smart as paint, and as cold and as hard as polished granite.

She had certainly made use of my money.

I crossed the room, pulled up a chair and sat down opposite her.

As I did so, the big man, sitting in the corner, moved around slightly and stared fixedly at me. I knew then he was Rima's bodyguard.

"Hello," Rima said, and opening her lizard skin bag she took out my letter and tossed it across the table at me.

"What's this all about?"

I screwed up the letter and put it in my pocket.

"You have had ten thousand. That will have to hold you. I can't spare any more for the time being. I need all the money I have to save my wife's life."

She took out a flat, gold cigarette case from her bag, lifted out a cigarette and set it alight with a gold Dunhill lighter.

"Looks like you and me are going to jail then," she said. "I told you:I don't give a damn one way or the other. I should imagine you would want to be with your wife, but if you want to go to jail I can fix it for you."

"You can't mean that" I said. "I need every dollar I have to take care of my wife. At the end of the month I'll give you something. I don't know how much, but it'll be something. That's the best I can do."

She laughed.

"You'll do much better than that, Jeff. You're going to give me a cheque for ten thousand right now, and on the first of the month another cheque for thirty thousand. Those are the terms. I need the money. If I don't get it, I'm ready to go to jail. If I go to jail, you'll come with me. Please yourself."

I stared at her. The burning desire that was in me to destroy her must have shown on my face, for she suddenly giggled. .

"Oh, I know. You would like to kill me, wouldn't you? But don't kid yourself," she said. "I'm much too smart. Do you see that poor ox, sitting over there in his finery? He's in love with me. He doesn't ask questions. He does what I tell him. He's just a dumb, blind ox, but he's tough. Don't kid yourself you could tangle with him. He's never more than ten feet away from me. You won't be able to kill me even if you find me, and you won't even be able to do that. So forget about it."

"You don't seem to understand my position," I said, trying to speak calmly. "My wife has had a serious accident and she is dangerously ill. I have a lot of unexpected expenses coming up. All I'm asking is for time to pay you. I can't give you any money now and still take care of the doctors' bills."

"Can't you?" She leaned back in her chair, lifting her eyebrows. "Well, all right, then I must go to the police. I either get the money or you go to jail. Please yourself."

"Now, listen . . ."

"You listen!" She leaned forward and her expression was suddenly vicious. "You seem to have a short memory! A little scene like this took place eleven years ago! Maybe you've forgotten it, but I haven't. We sat side by side in a car. You said unless I gave you thirty dollars you would take me to the police. Remember? You took my purse and everything I owned. You dictated to me! You told me I would have to work for you until the money was paid. I haven't forgotten! I warned you I wouldn't and I haven't! I promised myself if ever I got you in the same spot, I'd have as much mercy on you as you had for me! I don't give a damn about your wife! I don't give a damn about you, so save your breath! I want ten thousand dollars from you right now, and if I don't get it, I'm going to the police!"

Looking at her hard, degenerate face, I could see nothing I could say would light any spark of mercy in her. For a brief moment I was tempted to tell her to go to hell, but that was only for a brief moment. She was a junky. Her mind was unpredictable. I didn't dare call her bluff. She might go to the police, and if she did, I was sure they would come for me within a few hours of her giving them the information. There was no way out of this situation. She had me over a barrel. I would have to pay her.

I wrote the cheque and pushed it across the table to her.

"There it is," I said, and I was surprised how steady my voice sounded. "Now I'll give you a warning. You are right that I plan to kill you. One of these days I will find and kill you. Remember that."

She giggled.

"Stop talking like a movie script, and don't forget I want thirty thousand on the first of the month. If I don't get it, you won't hear from me, but you will hear from the cops."

I got to my feet. Out of the corner of my eye I saw her boy friend had also stood up.

"Don't say I didn't warn you," I said, and turning I crossed the bar to a row of telephone booths. I called the hospital and told the receptionist I was now on my way home.

"Oh, Mr. Halliday, will you hold on a moment... ?"

I was feeling pretty flat, but the sharp note in her voice brought me alert.

I heard her say something as if talking in an undertone to someone near by, then she said, "Mr. Halliday? Dr. Weinborg would like you to come in. There's nothing to be alarmed about, but he would like to see you as soon as possible."

"I'm coming," I said, and hung up.

I left the bar and in the street I waved to a cruising taxi. I told the driver to take me to the hospital fast.

As the cab drew away from the kerb, I caught sight of Rima and her boy friend walking towards the car park. She was looking up at him and smiling and he was staring hungrily down at her.

I reached the hospital in under seven minutes and I was shown straight into Dr. Weinborg's office.

He came around his desk and shook hands with me.

"Mr. Halliday, I'm not too satisfied with your wife's progress," he said. "She should be showing some improvement by now, but frankly, she isn't. Don't misunderstand me. Her condition hasn't deteriorated, but it hasn't improved, and in a case like this we look for improvement within three or four days of the operation."

I began to say something but found my lips so dry I couldn't get the words out. I just stared at him, waiting.

"I've talked to Dr. Goodyear. He suggests that Dr. Zimmerman should see your wife."

"What makes him imagine Dr. Zimmerman whoever he is can do anything better than he has done?" I asked.

Weinborg moved a letter opener around on his desk.

"Dr. Zimmerman is the most able specialist to do with the nerves of the brain, Mr. Halliday. He..."

"I thought Goodyear was that."

"Dr. Goodyear is a brain surgeon," Weinborg said patiently. "He doesn't handle post-operative cases. Dr. Zimmerman usually takes over from him in complicated cases."

"One clearing up the other's messes?"

Dr. Weinborg frowned.

"I understand how you must be feeling, but that is scarcely a fair thing to say."

"I suppose it isn't." I sat down abruptly. I was suddenly deadly tired and felt defeated. "Well, all right, let's get Dr. Zimmerman."

"It's a little more involved than just that," Weinborg said. "Dr. Zimmerman will only treat a patient if the patient is at his sanatorium out at Holland Heights. I'm afraid this will be an expensive business, Mr. Halliday, but I have every confidence that if your wife went to Dr. Zimmerman's place she would have the very best chance of recovery."

"Which is another way of saying if she remains here she doesn't stand such a good chance."

"That is correct. Dr. Zimmerman..."

"What will it cost?"

"That's something you will have to discuss with Dr. Zimmerman. At a guess about three hundred dollars a week. She would be under Dr. Zimmerman's personal supervision."

I lifted my hands despairingly. This thing seemed to be going on and on, making inroads into my money.

"Okay, let Dr. Zimmerman see her," I said. "When he's here I'll talk to him."

"He'll be here at eleven o'clock tomorrow morning."

Before I returned home, I looked in on Sarita. She was still unconscious. I took away with me a picture of her that crushed me.

When I got home I made a check on my financial position. With more expense ahead of me, it would be impossible to pay Rima any more money. I had four weeks ahead of me to find and silence her. Even if it meant leaving Sarita for a few days, I would have to do it.

The next morning I met Dr. Zimmerman. He was a middle-aged man with a lean face and keen eyes and a quiet, confidential manner. I liked him on sight.

"I've examined your wife, Mr. Halliday," he said. "There can be no question but she must come to my sanatorium. I am sure I can start good progress moving. The operation has been successful, but certain nerves have been damaged. However, these I think I can fix. In three or four months' time, when she is stronger, I'm going to talk to Dr. Goodyear and I'm going to suggest another operation. I think between the two of us we can certainly save her memory and we might even get her walking again, but she must be moved to my place immediately."

"What's it going to cost?"

"Three hundred a week for a private room. There will be nursing fees: say three hundred and seventy a week?"

"How about the second operation?"

"I couldn't say, Mr. Halliday. To be on the safe side, perhaps three thousand, possibly four."

I was beyond caring now.

"Go ahead," I said, paused and then went on, "I need to leave town for four or five days. When do you think my wife will be safe for me to leave?"

He looked a little surprised.

"It's too early for that. I'll be better able to tell in a couple of weeks. She won't be off the danger list until then."

So I waited two weeks.

I went back to the office and slaved to get ahead with the work so when the all-clear came I would be free to go on my hunt for Rima.

Ted Weston, the new man Jack had found to work with me, was keen and reliable. I had no misgivings once I had set him a programme that he wouldn't be able to carry it out.

Very slowly Sarita began to make progress. Each week I parted with three hundred and seventy dollars. My bank balance shrank. But I didn't regret the money because I now felt if anyone could pull her through it would be Zimmerman.

Finally I got a telephone call.

Zimmerman himself came on the line.

"You want to get off on business, Mr. Halliday? I think I can let you go now. There is a definite improvement in your wife's condition. She is not conscious yet, but she is much stronger, and I think you can go without any need to worry. It would be wiser to let me know where I can contact you just in case of a setback. This I don't anticipate, but it is well to be on the safe side."

I said I would let him know how to reach me, then after a few more words I hung up.

I sat staring in front of me, my heart thumping, and there came a cold feeling of triumph rising in me. At last after all these horrible, endless weeks, I could go after Rima.

I had thirteen days in which to find her before the thirty thousand had to be paid.

I was well ahead with my work. I could leave without throwing any extra work on Jack.

I caught a plane to Santa Barba the following morning.

103

CHAPTER FIVE

I

THE fat woman at the hotel opposite the Pacific & Union Bank recognised me as I walked up to the reception desk.

She gave me her dismal smile of welcome, saying, "It's a pleasure to see you again, Mr. Masters. If you want your old room, it's free."

I said I wanted it, passed a remark about the weather, added casually that I had a lot of work to do and wouldn't be leaving my room all day during my three-day stay, and then humped my bag up to the room.

The time was twenty minutes past one. I had brought a pack of sandwiches with me and a half bottle of Scotch, and I settled down at the window.

This seemed the bank's busiest time. Several people went in and out, but I didn't see Rima. I knew I was gambling on a long chance. It might be that she only came to the bank once a week or even once a month, but there was just no other way I could think of to get at her.

When the bank closed, still without my seeing Rima, I went down to the lobby and put through a long distance call to Zimmerman's sanatorium. I gave the receptionist there the telephone number of the hotel. I told her as I was almost certain to be out most of the time would she ask for Mr. Masters, who was a friend of mine, and who would pass on any message.

She said she would and then went on to say Sarita was still gaining strength although she was still unconscious.

It was a cold, blustery evening with a hint of rain in the air. I put on my raincoat, turned up the collar, pulled my hat down over my face and went out onto the streets.

I knew this was a risky thing to do, but the thought of spending the rest of the evening in this depressing hotel was more than my taut nerves could stand.

I hadn't gone far before it began to rain. I went into a movie house and sat through a dreary, fourth rate Western before returning to the hotel for dinner. I then went up to bed.

The next day followed exactly the same pattern. I spent all day at the window, not seeing Rima; the evening in a movie house.

That night, when I returned to the hotel, I felt a prick of panic. Was the trip going to fail? Time was moving on. I now had only eleven more days to find her, and these days could easily be the same as the previous days.

Although I went to bed, I found it impossible to sleep, and around twenty to one in the morning, unable to lie any longer in this box of a room, I got up, dressed and went down into the dimly lit lobby.

The old negro night watchman blinked sleepily at me when I told him I was going for a walk in the rain.

Grumbling under his breath, he unlocked the door and let me out.

There were a few cafe bars still open, and one or two dance halls, their red and blue neon lights making patterns on the sidewalk.

Young couples moved along in their plastic slickers, arm in arm, oblivious of the rain. A solitary cop balanced himself on the edge of the kerb, resting his aching feet.

I walked down to the sea, my hands thrust deep into the pockets of my raincoat, feeling a slight relaxing of my nerves in the chilly wind and rain.

I came upon one of the many sea food restaurants, built on piles over the sea. There was a long line of parked cars outside, and I could hear the strains of dance music. I paused to look down the long walk-in that led to swing doors and into the restaurant.

I was about to move on when a big man came out of the restaurant and ran down the wooden pier towards me, his head bent against the rain.

As he passed under one of the overhead lamps I recognised the cream sports coat and the bottle green slacks.

It was Rima's boy friend!

If it hadn't been raining and if he hadn't been running with his head down, he must have seen me and possibly recognised me.

I turned quickly so my back was to him, took out a pack of cigarettes and went through the motions of pretending to get a light in the wind.

Then I half turned to watch him.

He was leaning into a Pontiac convertible, groping in the glove compartment.

I could hear him swearing under his breath. He found what he was looking for, swung round and ran back down the pier and into the restaurant.

I stood looking after him. Then I walked casually over to the Pontiac and looked it over. It was a 1957 job, and not in too good condition. I glanced to right and left. There was no one in sight. Quickly, I picked hold of the licence tag on the steering wheel and flicked my cigarette lighter alight. I read the neatly printed name and address:

> *Ed Vasari*
> *The Bungalow*
> *East Shore, Santa Barba.*

I moved away from the car, then crossing over to a cafe opposite the restaurant, I pushed open the door and stepped in. There were only four teenagers sitting over cokes at one end of the room. I took a table by the window where I could see the Pontiac and sat down.

A tired looking waitress sauntered over and I ordered a coffee.

Was Rima with this man? Was she living with him at this address?

I sat there smoking and stirring my coffee, my eyes never off the Pontiac across the way. The rain increased and spattered against the window.

The four teenagers ordered another round of cokes. One of them, a blonde with a pert, knowing expression, wearing skin tight jeans and a sweater that showed off her immature childish shape, came over to where I was sitting and fed coins into the juke box.

The Platters began their soft moaning, and the teenagers joined in.

Then I saw them.

They came running out of the restaurant. Vasari was holding an umbrella over Rima. They dived into the Pontiac and drove off. If I hadn't been watching closely I would have missed them. They had come and gone so quickly.

Without drinking the coffee, I paid the waitress and walked out into the wet and the dark.

I was coldly excited and determined not to waste any time.

I walked fast to an all-night garage I had spotted on my way from the hotel. I went in there, and after a brief talk with one of the staff, I hired a Studebaker, paid the deposit, and while he was filling the car with gas I asked him casually where East Shore was.

"Turn right and keep going, following the sea," he told me. "It's about three miles from here."

I thanked him, then getting into the car, I drove out into the rain.

East Shore turned out to be a mile-long strip of beach with about thirty or forty wooden cabins dotted along the road.

Most of them were in darkness, but here and there lights showed.

I drove at a crawl along the road, staring at each cabin as I passed.

I could see nothing in the darkness that indicated any bungalow, and just as I was beginning to think I would have to leave the car and walk back, examining each cabin more closely, I saw ahead of me a light coming from a much more isolated building.

I drove towards it, then feeling sure this must be the place I pulled off the road, turned off the lights and got out of the car.

The rain, driven by the stiff sea breeze, beat against me, but I scarcely noticed it.

I approached the lighted window, and as I drew nearer I saw this place was a bungalow.

I paused at the double wooden gates. On the drive-in stood the Pontiac. I looked up and down the road, but as far as I could see there was no sign of life.

Cautiously, I opened the gate and walked up the drive-in.

There was a concrete path running around the bungalow and I followed it to the lighted window.

My heart was thumping hard now as I moved up to the window. I looked in.

The room was reasonably large and furnished reasonably well There were comfortable, but shabby lounging chairs, and a few modern, bright prints on the walls. There was a television set in a corner and a well stocked bar in another corner.

All this I took in at a glance, then my eyes rested on Rima.

She was sprawling in a low armchair, a cigarette between her lips, a glass of Scotch and water in her hand. She was wearing a green wrap that gaped open so I could see her long, slim legs which were crossed. One of them swung nervously and irritably as she stared up at the ceiling.

So she did live here! She did live with Vasari!

I watched her.

Suddenly the door pushed open and Vasari came in.

He was wearing a pair of pyjama trousers and he was naked to the waist. His great barrel of a chest was covered with coarse black hair and his tremendously developed muscles moved under his tanned skin as he rubbed the back of his head with a towel.

He said something to her and she looked at him, her expression hostile. She finished her drink, put the glass down and got to her feet. She stood for a moment, stretching, then she walked past him out of the room.

He snapped off the light and I found myself staring at my faint reflection in the rain-soaked window.

I moved away.

Further along, another window had lit up, but a blind covered it. I waited.

After some moments the light went out. The whole bungalow was now in darkness.

As silently as I had come, I returned to the Studebaker.

I got in and started the engine, then drove slowly back to my hotel.

While I drove, my mind was busy.

At last I had found her!

But there were still difficulties ahead. Did Vasari know she was blackmailing me? When I had got rid of her would I then have to deal with him?

It was while I was driving through the dark, wet night that I suddenly realised what I was planning to do. I was going to murder her. A cold feeling of fear took hold of me. It had been easy enough to tell myself she had to be silenced when I had found her, but now I had found her the thought of walking in on her and murdering her brought me out in a clammy sweat.

I pushed the thought out of my mind. It had to be done. First, I would have to get rid of Vasari. With him around I wouldn't be able to silence Rima. I decided I would have to watch the bungalow for a couple of days: I would have to find out what they did, how they lived and if Vasari ever left her alone.

I didn't sleep much that night.

The nightmare thought of what I had to do lay heavily on me.

II

A little after half past seven the following morning I was once again driving out to East Shore. I was confident I was safe to approach the bungalow in daylight at this hour. I couldn't imagine either of them would be early risers.

I drove past the bungalow fast. The blinds were drawn and the Pontiac still stood on the drive-in.

In the hard light of the morning sun the bungalow looked shabby: a typical sea-side vacation place, let year after year by an owner who never bothered to look at the place nor spare any money for a coat of paint.

Beyond the bungalow were sand dunes. After driving a few hundred yards further up the beach road I left the car behind a screen of shrubs and walked back towards the bungalow.

Within a hundred yards of the place was a line of dunes that offered excellent cover. From behind them I could watch the bungalow without being seen.

I had brought with me a pair of powerful field glasses I had been lucky enough to borrow from the owner of my hotel.

I made myself comfortable. By scooping away some of the sand, I was able to lie down against the face of the dune and rest the field glasses on top of it.

I watched the bungalow for more than an hour without seeing any sign of life.

At twenty minutes to nine, a battered old car came churning up the road and pulled up outside the bungalow. A woman got out. She walked up the path. I examined her through the glasses. They were so powerful I could see the smudges of powder on her face where she had put the powder on too thickly.

I guessed she was the maid, coming to clean up, and through the glasses I saw her dip two fingers into the mail box slot and then fish out a long string at the end of which was a key. She unlocked the front door with the key and entered the bungalow.

The long wait had paid off. I now knew how to get into the bungalow if I wanted to get in.

From time to time, through the big window, I caught sight of the woman moving about in the lounge. She was pushing an electric cleaner. After some minutes, she disconnected the cleaner and went away out of sight.

Time crawled by.

A little after eleven thirty the front door opened and Vasari came out. He stood on the step staring up at the sky, flexing his muscles and breathing in the fresh morning air. The sun was hot after the night's rain. He was wearing blue cotton slacks and a sweater shirt. He looked very massive. As a bodyguard he was impressive.

He went over to the Pontiac and checked the oil and water, then he returned to the bungalow.

It wasn't until midday that I saw Rima. She came to the front door and looked up at the sky. It was startling to put the field glasses on her face. She looked pale, and there were smudges under her eyes, and the rouge she had put on made her face look like a painted mask. Her expression was sullen. She got into the Pontiac and slammed the door viciously.

Vasari came out, carrying bathing wraps and towels. The cleaning woman came to the door. He said something to her and she nodded, then he got into the car and drove away.

I followed the car through the field glasses. It headed in the direction of the West side of the town where the swank beach clubs were.

A few minutes later the woman came out, locked the front door, dropped the key through the mail slot, got in her car and drove away.

I didn't hesitate.

This was an opportunity too good to miss. There was a chance that Rima kept the gun that had killed the guard in the bungalow. If I could get it, the case against me would be considerably weakened.

Before moving from my hiding place I examined the road and the beach carefully. There was no one in sight. I came out from behind the sand dunes and walked fast to the bungalow.

I opened the gate and walked up the drive-in. To be on the safe side, I rang the bell, although I knew there was no one in the place. After waiting a few minutes I fished up the key and opened the door. I stepped into the small hall and paused to listen. There was no sound except the busy ticking of a clock somewhere in the bungalow and the drip-drip-drip of a faulty tap in the kitchen.

The lounge was to my right. A short passage to my left led to the bedrooms.

I walked down the passage, opened a door and glanced into a room. This would be Vasari's dressing-room. A pair of slacks were neatly folded on a chair and an elastic shaver lay on the dressing-table. I didn't go in, but moved to the next door, opened it and stepped in side.

There was a double bed by the window and the dressing-table was loaded with cosmetics. A green silk wrap hung behind the door.

This was the room I wanted. I half closed the door, then went over to the chest of drawers and began going through the contents quickly, being careful not to disturb anything.

Rima had been on a buying spree with my money. The drawers were crammed with nylon underwear, scarves, handkerchiefs, stockings and so on. I didn't find the gun.

I turned my attention to the closet. A dozen or so dresses hung on hangers, and on the floor of the closet was a number of pairs of shoes. On the top shelf I saw a cardboard box tied with string. I took it down, slid off the string and opened the box. It contained letters and a number of photographs, most of them of Rima with her silver hair, taken at the film studios.

A letter on the top of the pile caught my attention. It was dated three days ago. I picked it from the box and read it.

234 Castle Arms,

Ashby Avenue,

San Francisco.

Dear Rima,

Last night I ran into Wilbur. He is out on parole and he is looking for you. He is on the stuff again and he is dangerous. He told me if he finds you he'll kill you. So watch out. I told him I thought you were in New York. He is still here, but I am hoping he will go off to New York. If he does so, I'll let you know. Anyway, you keep clear of here. He gives me the creeps and he means what he says about fixing you.

In a rush to catch the mail.

Clare.

I had completely forgotten Wilbur's existence.

My mind flashed back to Rusty's bar. I saw again the door slamming open and the sudden appearance of the small nightmare figure. Dangerous? An understatement. Then he had been as deadly as a rattlesnake as he had moved to where Rima had been crouching, the flick knife in his hand.

So he was out of jail after thirteen years, and he was looking for Rima.

When he found her he would kill her.

A tremendous surge of relief ran through me. This might be my way out: the solution to my problem.

I copied the woman Clare's address into my pocket diary and replaced the letter in the box and the box in the cupboard.

Then I continued my search for the gun, my mind busy.

It was by chance I found the gun. It was hanging by a string inside one of Rima's dresses. It was only because I impatiently pushed aside the row of dresses to look behind them that I felt it.

I untied the string and lifted the gun clear.

It was a .38 Police Special, and it was loaded. I slid the gun into my hip pocket, shut the cupboard and looked around the room to make sure I had left no signs of my search, then satisfied, I crossed the room to the door.

As I opened the door I heard a car pull up outside the bungalow.

I jumped to the window, my heart beginning to thump. I was in time to see Rima getting out of the Pontiac. She ran up the drive-in and I heard her fumbling for the key.

As the key grated in the lock I moved silently and swiftly out of the bedroom. I paused for a split second in the passage, then stepped into Vasari's dressing-room. I pushed the door to as the front door opened.

Rima walked quickly past the dressing-room and into her bedroom

I stood against the wall so that if Vasari opened the door it would conceal me as it swung back. I was tense and scared, and my heart was pounding.

I heard Vasari come heavily into the hall. There was a pause, then I heard him walk into the lounge. After a few minutes Rima left her bedroom and joined him in the lounge.

"Look, baby," he said in a complaining voice, "can't you lay off the stuff? For the love of Mike? We no sooner go somewhere when you have to come rushing back for a shot."

"Oh, shut up!" Rima's voice sounded vicious and harsh. "I do what I like here and don't you forget it!"

"Oh, sure, but why the hell don't you carry the stuff around with you if you've got to have it? You've balled up the whole day now."

"I told you to shut up, didn't I?"

"I heard you. You're always telling me to shut up. I'm getting sick of it."

She laughed.

"That's a joke! What are you going to do about it, then?"

111

There was a long pause, then he said, "Who's this guy you're getting money from? He worries me. What's he to you?"

"He's nothing to me. He owes me money and he pays me. Will you shut up about him?"

"How comes he owes you money, baby?"

"Look, if you don't stop this you can get out. You hear me?"

"Now, wait a minute." His voice hardened. "I'm in enough trouble as it is. I tell you this guy worries me. I think you're blackmailing him, and that's something I don't go for."

"Don't you?" Her voice was sneering. "But you don't mind stealing, do you? You don't mind knocking some old guy on the head and taking his roll, do you?"

"Cut that out! If they caught me I'd go away for a year, but blackmail ... hell! They give you ten years for that!"

"Who says anything about blackmail? I told you he owes me money."

"If I thought were were blackmailing him, baby, I'd leave you."

"You? Leave me? That's a laugh. You watch your step, Ed. Two can make threats. What's to stop me telephoning the cops and telling them where you are? Oh, no, you won't leave me."

There was a long pause.

In the silence I could hear the clock ticking.

Then Vasari said uneasily, "You always talk crazy after a shot. Forget it. So long as you know what you are doing. You wouldn't touch blackmail, baby, would you?"

"I'm not talking crazy!" she snapped. "If you don't like the way I live, you can get out! I can get on without you, but I'm damn sure that you can't get on without me!"

"This guy has me worried, Rima." His voice was now hesitant. "He's giving you plenty, isn't he? How comes he owes you all this dough?"

"Shut up about him! You heard what I said: do you want to get out or do you want to stay?"

"I don't want to get out, baby, I love you. Just so long as I know you're not cooking trouble for us, I don't mind."

"There's going to be no trouble. Come here and kiss me."

"You're sure about the trouble? This guy wouldn't...."

"Come here and kiss me."

I opened the door silently and stepped into the passage. I heard Rima moan softly as I moved down the passage and into the kitchen. I unlocked the door that led out onto the veranda, and then shutting it silently behind me, I ran back to the cover of the sand dunes.

I lay against the sand bank and watched the bungalow. It wasn't until after four o'clock that they came out and got into the Pontiac. When they had driven away I got to my feet.

Well, at least I had the gun. I knew now that Vasari wasn't in on Rima's blackmail racket. It was a safe bet that no one else shared her information about me. I knew Wilbur was out of jail and hunting for her.

My problems were becoming simplified. If I could find Wilbur and tell him where Rima was he would wipe her out for me.

There were still difficulties. If she found the gun had vanished, would she get into a panic and leave the bungalow and go into hiding? I decided there was a reasonable chance that she wouldn't discover that I had taken the gun. How long did she intend staying in the bungalow? That was something I had to find out. It might take me some time to find Wilbur. I had to be sure she would still be in the bungalow when I found him.

I returned to my hotel. I called the biggest real estate agent in town and told him I was interested in renting the bungalow on East Shore. Did he know when it would be vacant? He said it was let for the next six months. I thanked him, and said I would look in next time I was passing to see if he had anything else to offer. Then I hung up.

If Rima didn't discover the loss of the gun she would obviously remain in the bungalow for as long as was necessary. I now had to find Wilbur.

I called the sanitorium and asked after Sarita. The nurse said she was still making progress and there was no need for me to be anxious. I told her I had to go to San Francisco, and would let her know where to contact me, then I settled my account with the hotel, returned the Studebaker to the garage and took a train to San Francisco.

I hadn't much to go on: a woman's first name, her address and the knowledge that Wilbur had been seen in this city.

That was all, but if I had any luck it could be enough.

I told a taxi driver to take me to a hotel near Ashby Avenue.

He said there were three hotels on Ashby Avenue itself, and his choice, for what it was worth, would be the Roosevelt. I told him to take me there.

When I had booked in and had had my suitcase taken up to my room, I left the hotel and walked past the Castle Arms.

This turned out to be a big apartment block that had seen better days. Now its ornate brasswork was tarnished and its paintwork dilapidated.

I caught a glimpse of the janitor as he aired himself at the main entrance. He was a little man in a shabby uniform, and he had forgotten to shave this day. The kind of man who could use a dollar without asking questions.

I tramped the streets for the next half-hour until I came upon one of those printing-while-you-wait establishments. I asked the clerk in charge to print me some cards. I wrote down what I wanted

H. Masters.
Insurance and Credit Investigator.
City Agency, San Francisco.

He said he would have the cards ready within an hour. I went over to a nearby cafe and read the evening paper and drank two cups of coffee.

Then I collected the cards, and a little before nine o'clock I walked into the lobby of the Castle Arms.

There was no one behind the reception desk nor anyone to take care of the elevator. A small sign with an arrow pointing to the basement stairs told me where I could find the janitor.

I went down and knocked on a door at the foot of the stairs. The door opened and the shabby little man I had seen airing himself looked suspiciously at me.

I poked my card at him.

"Can I buy a few minutes of your time?" I said.

He took the card, stared at it, then gave it back to me.

"What was that?"

"I want some information. Can I buy it from you?"

I had a five dollar bill in my hand. I let him see it before returning it to my pocket.

He suddenly became friendly and eager.

"Sure, come on in, friend," he said. "What do you want to know?"

I entered the tiny room that served as an office. He sat down on the only chair. After pushing aside a couple of brooms and lifting a pail on to the floor, I found a seat on an empty wooden crate.

"Information about a woman staying here," I said. I took out the five dollar bill and folded it, keeping it before him. He stared hungrily at it. "She's in apartment 234."

"You mean Clare Sirns?"

"That's the one. Who is she? What does she do for a living?"

I gave him the bill which he hurriedly pushed into his hip pocket.

"She's a stripper at the Gatsby Club on MacArthur Boulevard," he told me. "We have plenty of trouble with her. It's my guess she's a junky. The way she behaves sometimes, you'd imagine she was crazy. The management has warned her! if she doesn't quit making trouble she'll have to leave."

"Not a good credit bet?"

"The worst I'd say," he said shrugging. "If you're thinking of talking to her, watch out. she's a toughie."

"I don't want to talk to her," I said, getting to my feet. "If she's like that, I don't want to have anything to do with her."

I shook hands with him, thanked him for his help and left. I returned to my hotel, changed, then took a taxi to the Gatsby Club.

There was nothing special about it. You can find a club like the Gatsby in any big town. It is always in a cellar. It always has an ex-pug as a doorman-cum-bouncer. It always has dim lighting and a small bar just inside the lobby. There are always hard-faced, bosomy girls hanging around the bar waiting for an invitation to a drink and who will go to bed with you later for three dollars if they can't get more.

I paid the five dollars' entrance fee, signed the book in the name of Masters and went into the restaurant.

A slim girl, wearing a tight-fitting evening dress that hinted she hadn't anything else on under it, her black hair falling to her shoulders and her grey-blue eyes full of silent and worldly invitation, came over to me and asked me if she could share my table.

I said not right now, but later I would buy her a drink.

She smiled sadly at me and went away, shaking her head at the other five unattached girls who were looking hungrily at me.

I had an indifferent dinner and watched a still more indifferent cabaret show.

Clare Sims did her strip act.

She was a big, generously built blonde with an over-developed bust and hip line that made the customers stare. There was nothing to her act except the revealing of a lot of flesh.

A little after midnight, just when I was thinking I had been wasting my time, there was a slight commotion at the door and a small dark-haired man came into the restaurant.

He was wearing a shabby tuxedo and heavy horn-rimmed spectacles.

He stood in the doorway, snapping his fingers and jerking his body in time with the music: a compact figure of evil.

He was gaunt and his hair was turning grey at the temples. His face was the colour of tallow. His lips were bloodless. The degeneracy in his face told its own story. I didn't have to look twice. It was Wilbur.

CHAPTER SIX

I

THE dark girl in the skin-tight dress who had spoken to me moved with a hip-swinging walk towards Wilbur, a professional smile on her red lips. She paused near him, her slim fingers touching her hair, her black pencil lined eyebrows lifted in invitation.

Wilbur continued to snap his fingers and weave his thin body in time with the music, but his owl-like eyes, glittering behind his glasses, shifted to the girl and his bloodless lips lifted off his teeth in a grimacing smile that meant nothing. Then, still snapping his fingers, he moved towards her and she too began to strut and stamp in time with the music.

They circled each other, waving their hands in the air, arching their bodies, postulating like two savages in a ritual dance.

The people in the restaurant paused in their eating and their dancing to stare at them.

Wilbur grabbed the girl's hand and twirled her around, sending her skirts flying out, revealing her long slim legs up to her thighs. He jerked her against him, then he shot her away from him at arm's length, jerked her back to him, twirled her again, then releasing her, he prowled around her, jiggling and stamping, until the band stopped playing.

Taking her arm in a possessive grip, he led her over to a table in a corner opposite mine and sat down with her.

I had been studying him. My first reaction at the sight of him when he had walked into the club was one of relief and triumph. But now, after watching him dancing, watching the cold, vicious face, my mind went back to that moment when he had come into Rusty's bar, knife in hand, and I saw again Rima's look of abject terror and heard again her screams.

This was my moment of hesitation. I had known when I had begun my hunt for her that my object was to kill her, but the full realisation, how it was to be done, was something I had avoided thinking about. I knew that although I had found her, I was sure if I had her alone in that bungalow I couldn't have steeled myself to murder her in cold blood. Instead, I had come in search of this man, knowing he wanted to kill her. I knew he would do it if he was told where she was. I had no doubt about that. There was something terrifying and deadly about him.

If I set this man on her, I would be responsible for her death; it wouldn't be an easy death; it would be a horrible one. Once I told him where he could find her, I would be signing her death warrant.

And yet if she didn't die, I would be saddled with her blackmailing threats for the rest of my days or until she did die. I would never shake her off.

"What is better than money?" she had said.

That was her philosophy. She had no mercy for me nor for Sarita: why then should I have any mercy for her?

I steeled myself. I would have to go ahead with this.

But before I told Wilbur where to find her, I had to get Vasari out of the way. There was a chance that Wilbur would be too quick for this ox of a man and would kill him if he tried to protect Rima. I wasn't going to be responsible for Vasari's death. I had nothing against him.

My first move was to find out where I could contact Wilbur. I had no intention of letting him know who I was. When I gave him Rima's address it would be over the telephone: an anonymous tip.

I then had to get Vasari out of the way. From the conversation I had overheard while he and Rima had been quarreling, the police were looking for him. Again an anonymous telephone call, warning him the police were coming for him, should send him on the run, but would Rima go with him?

The plan was complicated, but it was the best I could do. And time was running out. I now only had nine more days before I had to pay out the thirty thousand.

I watched Wilbur and the girl talking. He seemed to be trying to persuade her to do something. He leaned on the table, talking in a soft undertone, while he picked at a red pimple on his chin.

Finally, she shrugged impatiently, got up and walked over to the cloakroom.

Wilbur went over to the bar, ordered a Scotch which he tossed down and then moved over to the exit. The band was playing again, and as he left he snapped his fingers and waved his hands in time with the music.

I got my hat and raincoat from the hat check girl as the dark girl came out of the cloakroom, wearing a plastic mac over her evening dress.

She went out into the darkness with me just behind her.

I paused at the kerbside as if looking for a taxi. The girl hurried down the road. I could see Wilbur waiting for her. The girl joined him, and they crossed the road, walking quickly, and went up a side street.

I followed them, keeping in the shadows. At the corner I paused and looked cautiously around. I was in time to see the girl starting up the steps of an apartment house with Wilbur on her heels.

They disappeared from sight.

I didn't know if he was planning to stay the night with the girl, but I thought it was unlikely. I took up a position in a dark doorway and waited.

I waited half an hour, then I saw him come down the steps and saunter off down the road.

I went after him.

He wasn't difficult to follow. He didn't once look back, and he loitered along, whistling shrilly, and every now and then he went into a complicated dance step.

Finally he entered a dingy hotel near the waterfront. I paused and watched him through the glass panel door take a key off a rack and then wander out of sight up a steep flight of stairs.

I stepped back to read the overhanging sign: Anderson Hotel Restaurant.

I walked fast to the end of the street where I picked up a taxi and drove back to my hotel.

Was Wilbur staying at the hotel for the night or for longer? I couldn't risk losing him now I had found him.

But even then I found myself hesitating. Only the thought of Sarita and my urgent need to protect my money stiffened my nerves.

I went to a pay booth in the lobby, turned up the Anderson Hotel in the book and dialled the number.

After a while a girl said, "Yeah? What is it?"

I drew in a long deep breath. I had to make a conscious effort not to put the receiver back on its cradle.

"You got a little guy who wears glasses staying with you?" I said, making my voice sound tough.

"So what?" The girl's voice sharpened. "Who's calling?"

"A friend of his. Get him to the phone, sister, and hurry it up."

"If you're a friend of his, what's his name?"

"Stop talking so much. Get him to the phone."

"Oh, hang on," she said, her voice suddenly bored.

There was a long wait. I stood in the stuffy pay booth, the receiver clamped against my ear while I listened.

Five minutes dragged by, then I heard sounds. I heard the girl say angrily, "How do I know who it is? I keep telling you, don't I? Find out for yourself! " Then she gave a sudden squeal of pain'. "Oh! You dirty little rat! Keep your filthy paws off me!

I heard the receiver being picked up.

"Yeah? Who is it?"

I imagined him standing there, the light glittering on his spectacles, his white cruel face expectant.

"Wilbur?" I said.

"That's me. Who is it?"

Speaking slowly and distinctly, I said, "I saw Rima Marshal last night."

I heard him draw his breath in a tight little hiss.

"Who are you?"

"Never mind. Would you be interested to know where she is?"

I felt cold sweat on my face as I talked.

"Yeah. Where is she?"

"I'll send you her address in two days' time-on Friday morning, and some money to get to where she is," I said. "Stick around until Friday."

"Who the hell are you?" he demanded. "Are you a pal of hers ?

"Do I sound like a pal of hers?" I said, and hung up.

II

Early the next morning, from my hotel room, I put a call through to Dr. Zimmerman's sanatorium. The receptionist said Dr. Zimmerman wanted to talk to me and would I hold on?

When he came on the line, he sounded cheerful.

"I have good news for you, Mr. Halliday. Your wife is now making very steady progress. She has come out of her coma, and in a couple of days I think you can see her. We'll have to think about this second operation. When will you be back?"

"Sometime on Friday," I said. "I'll call you as soon as I get in. You really think she's over the worst now?"

"I'm sure she is. If you will come to the sanatorium on Saturday morning it is possible you can see her."

I said I would be along, and after some more talk I hung up.

The news that Sarita was so much better got me out of my mood of depression. My resolve to get rid of Rima began to weaken again.

Perhaps on Saturday I would be with Sarita. I would know while I stood by her bed that I had deliberately destroyed a life. I wondered how I would feel when our eyes met. Would she see the guilt in mine?

I got up and began to pace the floor. What right had I to take Rima's life? I asked myself. I was only destroying her to save myself going either to the gas chamber or to jail. Would I be able to live with myself if I were the direct cause of her death? This was a problem of conscience and it tormented me.

119

I looked for another solution. Suppose I refused to give Rima any more money-what then? I believed she would go to the police and I would be arrested. What would happen to Sarita without me? True, she would have my money, but how would she manage, alone and a cripple?

I tried to be honest with myself. Was I planning to get rid of Rima to save myself going to jail or because of Sarita's helplessness and her need for me?

I couldn't decide about this, but I did know Sarita needed me and I did know Rima's life was worthless.

I realised that my plan to get rid of her was as full of holes as a sieve. Even if I sent Wilbur her address, there was no guarantee that he would kill her. His hatred for her might already have petered out and he might not be bothered to make the journey. Also Vasari might not leave Rima after I had warned him the police were coming for him. If he did go, Rima might go with him and Wilbur would find the bungalow empty. If-if-ff...

As a murder plan it was completely cock-eyed.

It was at this moment that I decided to leave it cock-eyed. It would be like tossing a coin: heads-Rima dies: tails-I go to jail. That way I need not accept the entire blame if the plan happened to work and Rima died.

To get away from my thoughts, I went down to the breakfast room. I told the waitress to bring me coffee and toast. It was while I was waiting I glanced around the room. There were only eight or nine men eating breakfast: all obviously business men, intent on their food and their papers.

I became aware that one of them in a far corner had looked up and was staring intently at me. He was a fellow about my own age and his round, fleshy face was vaguely familiar. He got abruptly to his feet and came over, smiling at me. It wasn't until he had reached my table that I recognised him. He was a guy I had worked with at college, sharing the same room. His name was Bill Stovall and he had qualified as an engineer at the same time as I did.

"For the love of Mike!" he said. "It's Jeff Halliday, isn't it?"

I got to my feet and shook hands with him. He wanted to know what I was doing in San Francisco and I said I was up on a business trip. He said he had seen Life and had read about the bridge.

"You've certainly got a job there, Jeff! My goodness! Every damned engineer in the district has been after that one." We sat down and talked about the bridge. Then I asked him what he was doing.

"I'm with Fraser and Grant, the steel people. Incidentally, Jeff, we might be able to help you. You'll want steel and we can quote you figures that'll surprise you."

It suddenly occurred to me that if anything went wrong with my plan to get rid of Rima and it was traced back to me, it might be a sound idea to have a reason why I had come to San Francisco, so I said any figures on steel would interest me and how about it.

"Tell you what," he said, getting excited, "suppose you come along around half past ten and I'll introduce you to our steel man?" He gave me his card. "Will you do that?"

I said I would, and after telling me how to get to his place he went away.

I spent the morning and most of the afternoon with the steel man. The estimates he gave me were two per cent lower than anything I had had from other contractors. I promised to let him know as soon as I had consulted Jack.

I returned to the hotel a little after five o'clock and went up to my room. I took a shower, changed, then I sat at the writing-desk and wrote Rima's name and address in large block letters on a sheet of paper. This I put in an envelope together with three ten dollar bills. I addressed the letter to Wilbur, care of Amderson's Hotel.

I went down to the lobby and asked the porter the times of trains to Holland City. He said there was one out at twenty minutes past eight.

I bought a stamp from him and put it on the letter to Wilbur. It took a conscious effort to cross to the mail box and drop the letter in. As soon as I had done it, I felt the urge to have it back.

I went into the bar and had a drink. I was sweating slightly. By eight o'clock tomorrow morning Wilbur would get the letter. What would he do? If he really intended to murder Rima he could be in Santa Barba by half past two in the afternoon.

He was a junky, and therefore, like Rima, unpredictable. He could easily be tempted to spend the money I had sent him for his fare on drugs. The chances were he would remain in San Francisco and not go to Santa Barba.

With that thought to quell the pricking of my conscience, I went into the snack bar and ate a sandwich. Then I paid my bill, and while waiting for my suitcase to be brought down I shut myself in a pay booth. I asked 'Information' to give me the telephone number of The Bungalow, East Shore, Santa Barba. After the usual delay, she

121

told me it was East 6684. I wrote it down in my diary, then leaving the hotel I took a taxi to the station.

I arrived at Holland City soon after midnight. The ticket collector at the barrier grinned cheerfully at me.

"Nice to see you back, Mr. Halliday. Any good news of Mrs. Halliday?"

I said Sarita was making progress and I hoped to see her on Saturday.

"Glad to hear it," he said. "She's a fine lady, Mr. Halliday. I hope they put that bastard who ran into her away for years."

The taxi driver who drove me home also wanted to hear the latest news about Sarita. It suddenly dawned on me that she had become quite a public figure and that gave me a feeling of pride.

But I became terribly depressed when I unlocked the front door of my apartment and walked into the silent lounge. I paused for a long moment, half expecting to hear Sarita's voice greeting me. I felt very lonely as I looked at our familiar possessions, the clock that had stopped on the over-mantel, the film of dust on the television set.

I went into the bedroom, undressed, took a shower and put on my pyjamas. Then I went back to the lounge and mixed myself a stiff whisky and soda. I sat down by the telephone and lit a cigarette. When I had finished my drink and had stubbed out my cigarette I looked at my watch.

The time was now twenty minutes to two a.m. My mind went out into space to Santa Barba to the sordid little bungalow on East Shore. Rima and Vasari would be preparing for bed: maybe they would be in bed already.

I now had to go ahead with the second move in this plan of mine. I took up my pocket diary, lying on the table, checked the telephone number of the bungalow, then called 'Long Distance.' When the operator came on the line, I gave her the number. I said I would hold on.

I sat motionless, staring up at the ceiling, listening to the humming and the ghost voices that came to me over the open line. Then suddenly I heard the steady burr-burr-burr that told me the telephone bell was ringing.

It rang for some time, then there was a click and Rima's voice said angrily, "East 6684. Who is it?"

I felt my heart contract at the sound of her voice.

Making my voice hard and rough, I said, "Is Ed there?"

"Who's calling?"

The connection was so good I could hear her quick, uneven breathing.

"A pal of his. Never mind who it is. I want to talk to him."

"You don't talk to him unless you tell me who you are," she said, and I caught the note of uneasiness in her voice.

Then there was the sound of a sudden commotion.

I heard Rima say, "Don't be a fool, Ed!"

"Shut up!" I heard Vasari say. "I'll handle this!"

Then his voice barked in my ear: "Who is it?"

"Just a pal," I said, speaking slowly and distinctly. "You'd better beat it, Ed, and pronto. The cops spotted you this morning. By now they know where you are. They are waiting to get a warrant, then they're coming for you . . ."

I heard his quick intake of breath, and as he began to speak I hung up.

I sat there, my hand on the telephone receiver, staring across the room. For what it was worth, the stage was now set. Within six hours Wilbur would be opening my letter. He might or might not grab the first train to Santa Barba. If he did, I was pretty sure he would murder Rima, but in the meantime, Vasari might or might not go on the run. If he did, there was just that chance that Rima would go with him, so if Wilbur arrived he would find the bungalow deserted. On the other hand, Varasi might leave Rima, and Wilbur would find her. And yet again Vasari might not be stampeded and remain with Rima, in which case Wilbur would come up against some opposition. As a murder plan it was cock-eyed, but as a problem it did offer a number of solution. So many it was like the toss of a coin.

At least it was now out of my hands. I had set the stage and I would have to abide by the results.

I turned off the light and went into the bedroom. The empty bed alongside mine made me think of Sarita.

I wanted to pray for her, but the words wouldn't come.

I got into bed, but I didn't turn off the light. Darkness has a way of sharpening ones conscience.

CHAPTER SEVEN

I

SOON after six o'clock the next morning I drove down to the site of the bridge.

Already men were working and I had a brief word with the foreman. Jack had made tremendous progress since I had been away. The ground had been cleared either side of the river. A number of piles had already been sunk.

I prowled around, watching the men work for ten minutes or so, then I saw Jack's black and white Thunderbird coming fast down the hill. He pulled up near me, got out of the car and came over, his good-natured face split in a wide grin of welcome.

"Hi, Jeff! Good to see you. All fixed up?"

I shook his hand.

"Yes, all fixed up, and I have a surprise for you. I can get all the steel we want at two per cent under the best estimate we've already had."

He stared at me.

"Do you mean you've been working while you've been away? I thought you had gone on some private business."

"I'm always working," I said. "How do you like it, Jack? We make a saving of twenty five thousand."

"I like it fine! Tell me about it."

We talked business for the next twenty minutes, then he said, "We'd better talk to our contractors, Jeff. This is good news. Look, I have a couple of jobs here to do, then I'll be back at the office. See you then."

He walked over to my car with me. "And Sarita?" he asked.

"The news is good," I said. "I'm seeing Zimmerman tomorrow morning."

I told him about Zimmerman wanting to perform a second operation.

He listened sympathetically, but I could see the bridge was foremost in his mind, and I understood.

"That's fine, Jeff," he said. "Well, I guess...."

"Sure," I said. "I'll get over to the office. How is Weston shaping?".

"He's okay, but you're back in time, Jeff. He wants help, and I haven't time to give it to him."

"I'll take care of him."

"Fine. Okay, see you around eleven." and he went off, shouting to the foreman to come on over.

As I drove back to the office I looked at the clock on the dashboard. The time was seven forty five a.m. In another quarter of an hour Wilbur would get my letter. What would he do? I was aware that there was sudden sweat on my hands.

I parked the car, went up to the office where I found Ted Weston and Clara already at work.

They greeted me and then Clara gave me a pile of letters and documents, estimates and files.

I sat down and started in to work.

It wasn't until ten o'clock as I paused to light a cigarette that I suddenly remembered Wilbur. There was a train to Santa Barba at ten minutes past ten. Had he taken it? I had a sudden urge to find out.

I had already made a number of notes for Jack, and I pinned them together, then tossed them onto Weston's desk.

"Be a pal and take those down to Jack," I said. "He'll want them. I'll hold down this end."

"Why, sure, Mr. Halliday."

I looked at him.

He was a nice-looking kid, eager and right on the ball. The kind of youngster I wish I had been. I watched him pick up the notes and hurry out of the office. I watched him enviously. I wished I had been like him. With any luck at all, he wouldn't get a lump of red hot shrapnel in his face and spend months in a plastic surgery ward, listening to the groans and screams of those patients who just hadn't what it takes to accept a new face. He wouldn't tangle with a silver-headed, golden-voiced junky who could kill a man without blinking an eyelid. He wouldn't live under the threat of blackmail nor would he plan a murder... one of the lucky ones, and I envied him.

As soon as he had gone, I picked up the telephone receiver and asked Clara to give me an outside line. When I got it, I called 'Long Distance' and gave the girl the number of the Anderson Hotel. She told me the lines to San Francisco were busy, but she would call me back.

I sat smoking and sweating. I had to wait ten long, nerve-wracking minutes before I got through.

The same girl's indifferent voice demanded, "Yeah? What is it?",

"I want to talk to Wilbur," I said.

"Well, you can't. He's checked out." My heart gave a little lurch.

"You mean he's left?"

"What else do you think I mean?" "Do you know where he has gone?"

"No, and I don't care either," and she hung up.

I put down the receiver and taking my handkerchief from my pocket I wiped my face and hands.

So he had gone, but had he gone to Santa Barba? If he had, he couldn't get there until after two in the afternoon. I was in a sudden panic to stop this thing. All I had to do was to call Rima and warn her he was coming.

I very nearly did it, but at that moment the door jerked open and Jack, Weston and two contractors came in.

As I greeted the contractors I looked at my desk clock. The time was fifteen minutes past eleven. I still had time to warn Rima during the lunch hour.

But it so happened the session with the contractors became so involved that Jack suggested we should all lunch together and try to straighten out our problem while we eat.

"Look, you boys go on ahead," I said. "I have a telephone call to make, then I'll be with you."

When they had gone, I lit a cigarette and stared at the telephone. If I warned Rima that Wilbur was coming she would vanish. I would probably never find her again. She would continue to blackmail me, and if I didn't pay I would go to jail, but the thought of Wilbur, sitting in the train, getting nearer and nearer to her, turned my blood cold.

This cock-eyed murder plan was like the toss of a coin. Heads - she died. Tails—I went to jail. Why not decide it that way right now?

I took a coin out of my pocket, then flicked it high into the air. I heard it fall on the floor by my side. For several moments I sat there, not looking down, then with an effort I leaned forward and looked at the coin.

It lay heads up!

Well, there it was. I could wash my hands of the responsibility. I could let events take their course. I got to my feet, stubbed out my cigarette and started for the door.

Then I stopped.

Into my mind came the memories of Rusty's bar. I saw Wilbur again with the knife in his hand. I saw Rima crouching in the booth, her mouth open, and I heard again her scream of terror. I heard too the sound of her nails scratching on the wall.

I couldn't do this thing to her. I had to warn her.

I went back to the desk, picked up the telephone and called 'Long Distance.' I gave the girl Rima's telephone number.

I waited, listening to the humming over the open line.

The girl said, "There's no reply. Should there be one?"

"I guess so. Call them again, will you, please?"

There was another long wait, then the girl said, "I'm sorry, your party's not answering."

I thanked her and hung up.

The obvious thing had happened: Vasari had bolted, and Rima had gone with him.

II

But I didn't leave it like that. There was the chance, of course, that Rima had been out and would return later. Three times during the day, when Weston was out of the office, I called the bungalow, but there was still no answer.

Finally, I decided she had gone and this cock-eyed murder plan of mine to get rid of her by remote control had failed.

I was glad and relieved. Now, I would have to prepare for trouble. In six days' time Rima would be expecting thirty thousand dollars to be paid into her bank. I wasn't going to pay. What would she do? Go to the police? I couldn't take any chances. I had to assume she would go to the police, and very shortly I would be arrested for murder.

I now had to make arrangements for Sarita's future. I called Mayor Mathison and asked him if I could come around to his place after dinner.

He wanted me to come to dinner, but I made an excuse. I wasn't in the mood for that kind of an outing.

I found Helen and Mathison sitting before the fire and they welcomed me. I told them about the coming operation.

Mathison said at once, "How are you fixed for money, Jeff ? This could be an expensive business. You know how we both feel about Sarita. We look on her as our own daughter."

"Yes", I said. "The money's not the trouble. I can take care of that, but it certainly looks as if she will have to have a lot of care and attention for years. She has no one except me to rely on. If anything happened to me she would be alone."

"Of course she wouldn't," Mathison said. "Didn't I just say we looked on her as a daughter. If anything happened to you, she would come here to live. Anyway, what's all this? What is likely to happen to you?"

"I know how he feels," Helen broke in. "One never knows. He's right to be worried." She smiled at me. "We'll look after her, Jeff: that's a promise."

That was a tremendous burden off my mind. As I drove home I felt for the first time, since Rima had started to blackmail me, at ease in my mind.

The following morning I went to the sanatorium. Zimmerman told me Sarita was still making progress.

"I don't want to raise your hopes too much, Mr. Halliday," he said, "but there is a chance-not much of one-but a chance that if we have any luck she will walk again."

He took me to see Sarita. She looked very pale and small in the hospital bed. She was conscious and she recognised me, but she hadn't the strength to speak to me.

I was allowed to stand by her bed, looking at her for a couple of minutes, and in those minutes everything she meant to me came into sharp focus.

I was glad my plan to get rid of Rima had failed. I knew I couldn't have looked at Sarita the way I was looking at her now if I had been guilty of murder.

Jack and I spent the whole of Sunday and Monday on the bridge site. We had run into a snag of shifting soil, and we had to work out a way to handle it.

By Tuesday evening we had solved the problem. Wednesday and Thursday were days of hard slogging work at the office. I managed to get over to the sanatorium every evening to exchange smiles with Sarita. She still couldn't talk, but at least she recognised me.

On Friday, the day I should pay the money to Rima, Zimmerman called me around ten o'clock. He said Goodyear was with him and they had examined Sarita.

"We have decided not to wait, Mr. Halliday. We are operating tomorrow morning."

I said I would be there. I called Mayor Mathison and told him. He said it wouldn't be possible for him to get over to the sanatorium, but Helen would join me.

I went out in the evening to see Sarita, and for the first time she managed to say a few words.

"They're going to fix you up tomorrow, darling," I said to her. "You're going to be fine in a little while."

"Yes, Jeff ... I do want to get home."

On my way back to the apartment I thought by now Rima would know the money wasn't going to be paid. She would probably wait

a couple of days to be sure-then what would she do? But right then I had too much on my mind to bother much about her.

The operation began at eleven o'clock the following morning and lasted four hours. Helen and I sat in the waiting-room, not speaking, but every now and then she would smile at me and pat my hand.

A little after two o'clock a nurse came in and said my office was calling me. She said the operation was nearly over, and there would be news for me in about half an hour.

The telephone was down the corridor. It was Clara on the line.

"Oh, Mr. Halliday, I'm sorry to call you, but there is a Detective Sergeant Keary here. He says it is important he should talk to you."

I felt my heart give a little bounce and then began to race.

"He'll have to wait," I said. "The operation will be over in half an hour. I can't get back to the office before five. What's he want?"

I knew what he wanted all right. So Rima had gone to the police!

"If you'll hold on, Mr. Halliday, I'll ask him. . ."

Clara sounded slightly flustered.

There was a pause, then a man's voice said, "This is Detective Sergeant Keary, Santa Barba City police. I would like to see you just as soon as I can."

"What is it?" I said.

"Police business," he said curtly. "I can't talk on the telephone."

"Well, all right," I said, matching his tone. "You'll have to wait. I'll be back at five. I'll see you then," and hung up.

I wiped my sweating hands on my handkerchief. Had he a warrant for my arrest? Had they already arrested Rima?

I saw Zimmerman coming down the corridor. He was smiling

"Dr. Goodyear will be with you in a moment," he said. "He's just washing up. I have good news for you. We are practically certain the operation will be a success. Unless something goes very badly wrong, and we don't anticipate this, in a few months your wife will be walking again."

The next half hour was spent with Goodyear in a technical discussion that didn't mean much to me, but I did gather that with careful nursing, patience and many months, Sarita would get back to normal.

While Goodyear talked, I kept thinking of Detective Sergeant Keary waiting for me. Goodyear said in couple of days I would be able to see Sarita, but not before. I thought in a couple of days I would be in the Los Angeles jail.

I left the sanatorium with Helen.

"That talk we had yesterday about you and Ted taking care of

129

Sarita if anything happens to me," I said as I drove her down town.
"That still goes, doesn't it?"

"Why, of course, Jeff ..."

"I'm in a bit of a mess," I said, not looking at her. "I don't want
to go into details, but it could be I'll be out of circulation for some
time and I'm relying on you and Ted to stand by Sarita."

"Why not go into details, Jeff?" she said quietly. "You know how
Ted feels about you, and I feel that way too. If there is anything we
can do..."

"I just want to be sure Sarita is all right," I said. "You do that,
and you'll be doing everything."

She put her hand on mine.

"All right. You don't have to worry about Sarita, and Jeff, I'm
sorry ... Ted and I like you a lot."

I dropped her off at the City Hall. She wanted to tell Mathison
the news about Sarita. She looked through the car window at me and
smiled.

"Don't forget... anything we can do ..."

"I won't forget ...."

Ten minutes later I walked into my office.

Clara, busy thumping a typewriter, paused and looked at me.

"It's pretty good news," I said, taking off my raincoat. "They
think she'll walk again. It's going to take time, but they seem pretty
confident.

"I'm so glad, Mr. Halliday."

"Where's this police officer?"

"He's in your office. Mr. Weston had to go down to the site.
He's in there alone."

I crossed the room, turned the handle of the door and entered.

A large, heavily built man sat at ease in one of the leather
lounging chairs we had bought for important clients.

He had a typical cop face: red, fleshy and weather beaten with
the usual small hard eyes and the rat-trap mouth. He had bulky
shoulders and a bulky waistline, and his thinning hair was turning
grey.

As he heaved himself to his feet, he said, "Mr. Halliday?"

"That's right," I said and closed the door. My hands were damp
and my heart was thumping, but with a conscious effort I managed
to keep my face expressionless.

"I'm Detective Sergeant Keary, Santa Barba City police."

I went around my desk and sat down.

"I'm sorry to have kept you waiting, sergeant," I said. "Sit down.
What can I do for you?"

130

He sat down. The small green eyes worked over me.

"Just a routine investigation, Mr. Halliday. I'm hoping you can help us."

This was so unexpected I was off balance for a moment. I Was expecting to be arrested. I stared at him.

"Why, sure. What is it?"

"We are looking for a man known as Jinx Mandon. Does the name mean anything to you?"

A false alarm! A wave of relief ran over me. My tension relaxed.

"Jinx Mandon? Why no."

The small eyes continued to probe.

"Never heard of him?"

"No."

He took out a pack of chewing gum, stripped off the wrapping paper and put the gum in his mouth. His movements were slow and deliberate. He rolled the wrapping paper into a small ball and dropped it into the ash tray on my desk. All the time he stared fixedly at me.

"What's your home address, Mr. Halliday?"

I told him, wondering why he asked.

"What is all this about, anyway?" I said.

"Mandon is wanted for armed robbery." Keary's heavy jaws revolved on the gum. "Yesterday we picked up an abandoned car outside the Santa Barba railroad station. Mandon's fingerprints were on the steering wheel. The car had been stolen from Los Angeles. In the compartment we found a scrap of paper on which was written your name and address."

My heart gave a little kick against my side. Could Jinx Mandon be Ed Vasari? To cover my start of surprise, I opened the cigarette box on my desk, took out a cigarette and lit it.

"My name and address?" I said, desperately trying to sound casual. "I don't understand."

"It's simple enough, isn't it?" There was a sudden grating note in Keary's voice. "A car used by a wanted criminal has your name and address in the glove compartment. There's not much to understand about that. How do you account for it?"

I was recovering quickly.

"I don't account for it," I said. "I have never heard of this man."

"Maybe you have seen him."

He took from his pocket an envelope, and from the envelope a half plate glossy photograph which he flicked across the desk to me.

I was already braced as I looked at the photograph. It was Ed Vasari all right: there was no mistaking him.

131

"No," I said. "I don't know him."

Keary reached across the desk, picked up the photograph, returned it to the envelope and the envelope back into his pocket. His heavy jaws revolved on the gum as he continued to stare at me.

"Then why did he have your name and address in the car?"

"I wouldn't know. Maybe the owner of the car knows me. Who is he?"

"He doesn't know you. We have already asked him."

"Then I can't help you, sergeant."

He crossed one thick leg over the other, his jaws moving slowly and rhythmically on the gum.

"You're building a bridge, aren't you?" he asked, unexpectedly. "You had your picture in Life this week?"

"Yes. What has that to do with it?"

"Maybe Mandon got your name from the magazine. Was your address mentioned?"

"No."

He shifted his bulk in the chair, frowning.

"Quite a mystery, isn't it? I don't like mysteries. They make a report untidy. You have no idea why Mandon should have had your name and address in his car?"

"None at all."

He chewed for a moment or so, then shrugging his heavy shoulders he climbed to his feet.

"There must be some explanation, Mr. Halliday. You think about it. Maybe you'll remember something. If you do, give me a call. We want this guy, and were going to get him. There may be a hook-up between you and him you have forgotten."

"No chance of that," I said, getting up. "I don't know him and I've never seen him."

"Well, okay. Thanks for your time." He started towards the door, then paused. "Quite a bridge you're building."

"Yes."

"Is that right it'll cost six million bucks?"

"Yes."

He stared at me, his small eyes probing again.

"Pretty nice going, if you can get it," he said. "Well, so long, Mr. Halliday."

He nodded and went away.

I felt cold sweat on my face as I watched the door close silently after him.

CHAPTER EIGHT

I

The next two days were days of hard work and tension. I was continually expecting either Rima to telephone or the Los Angeles police to walk in and arrest me. At least, Sarita was making excellent progress: the only bright spot in those two days.

Then on Thursday morning, as Ted Weston and I were preparing to go down to the bridge site, Clara came in to tell me Detective Sergeant Keary was here again to see me.

I told Weston to go on ahead, and I would follow as soon as I could. When he had gone, I told Clara to show Keary in.

I sat at my desk, tense and aware that my heart was beating too fast.

Keary came in.

As he closed the door, I said, "I can't give you long, sergeant. I'm due at the bridge site. What is it this time?"

But he was a man no one could hustle. He settled his bulk in the armchair and pushed his hat to the back of his head. He then produced a pack of chewing gum and began to unwrap it.

"This guy Mandon," he said. "We now learn he went under another name: Ed Vasari. Ever heard of that name, Mr. Halliday?"

I shook my head.

"No. That name means nothing to me either."

"We're still puzzled why your name and address should have been in his car, Mr. Halliday. We think even if you don't know Mandon, he must have known you at some time or the other. We found out where he has been hiding: a small bungalow in Santa Barba. In the bungalow we found a copy of *Life* with your photograph in it. The photograph was ringed around in pencil. That, and the fact your name and address was in his car, suggests he either knew you or was interested in you, and we want to know why." He paused in his chewing to stare at me. "What do you think?"

"It puzzles me as much as it puzzles you," I said.

"You are sure you have never seen this man? Do you want another look at his photograph?"

"It's not necessary. I have never seen him before."

He scratched his ear and frowned.

"Like I said: a mystery. We don't like mysteries, Mr. Halliday."

I didn't say anything.

"Have you ever heard of a woman who calls herself Rima Marshall?"

133

Well, here it is, I thought. I was expecting the question but in spite of that I felt a sudden cold shrinking inside me.

I looked straight at him as I said, "No. I don't know her either. Who is she?"

"Mandon's girl friend," Keary said. "They lived together in this bungalow."

He chewed some more, his small eyes fixed in a blank stare at the ceiling.

After a long pause, I said sharply, "I told you I'm busy, sergeant. Is there anything else ?"

He turned his head and his eyes locked with mine.

"This woman has been murdered."

My heart skipped a beat and then began to race. I know I changed colour.

"Murdered?" I managed to say. "Who has been murdered?"

The hard, probing eyes made a slight advance into my defences.

"Rima Marshall. We showed Mandon's photograph around and yesterday evening we found a woman who had been doing the cleaning. Imagine a punk like Mandon having a woman to do his cleaning! She recognised him. She told us about this Rima Marshall, and she gave us the address of the bungalow Mandon had been using for his hideout. We went there. Mandon had blown, but we found the woman." He shifted the gum around in his mouth. "Not one of the nicest looking corpses I have seen. She had been hacked to death with a knife. The Medical Officer told us she had thirty-three stab wounds: ten of them could have been fatal. On the table was this copy of Life with your photograph ringed around in pencil."

I sat motionless, my hands in tight fists out of sight under the desk. So Wilbur had found her! And I was responsible! I felt cold sweat break out on my face.

"We have a pretty sensational case on our hands," Keary went on. "We're now wondering if she left this paper with your name and address on it in the car. She might have known you at one time or the other. Her name means nothing to you?"

"No."

He took an envelope from his pocket, From the envelope he took out a photograph and laid it on the desk.

"Maybe you might recognise her."

I looked at the photograph and then turned quickly away.

It was a horrible photograph.

Rima lay in a pool of blood on the floor. She was naked. Her body had been horribly cut, stabbed and mutilated.

"You don't recognise her?" Keary asked in his tough cop voice.

"No! I don't know her! I don't know Mandon! Is that clear?" I said. "I can't help you! Now will you please get out of here and let me get on with my work?"

But he wasn't a man to be bullied. He settled himself more firmly in his chair as he said, "This is a murder case, Mr. Halliday. Its your bad luck that in some way you are connected with it. Have you ever been to Santa Barba?"

I very nearly said I hadn't, but realised in time that I might easily have been recognised in the -town, and to deny being there could get me into serious trouble.

"Yes, I have," I said. "What of it?"

He was all cop now, leaning forward, his chin thrust out.

"When was that?"

"A couple of weeks ago."

"Can you get it nearer than that?"

"I was there on May 21st and again on June 15th."

He looked slightly disappointed.

"Yeah. We've already checked. You stayed at the Shore Hotel.,"

I waited, thankful I hadn't been caught in a lie.

"Can you explain, Mr. Halliday," he went on, "why a man in your position should stay at a joint like the Shore Hotel? Any particular reason?"

"I just don't happen to be fussy where I stay," I said. "It was the first hotel I came to so I stayed there."

"Why did you go to Santa Barba?"

"Why all these questions? What business is it of yours where I stay and why?"

"This is a murder case," he said. "I ask the questions: you answer them."

Shrugging, I said, "I had a lot of figures to prepare. I couldn't get any peace here what with the telephone and the contractors disturbing me so I went to Santa Barba. I thought the change of air would do me good."

Keary rubbed the end of his fleshy nose with the back of his hand.

"What made you book in under the name of Masters?"

I was ready for that one. My mind was now working and shade faster than his.

"When you have a photograph in *Life*, sergeant, you acquire a certain amount of notoriety. I was anxious not to be disturbed by the Press so I booked in under my mother's maiden name."

He stared at me, his hard green eyes as blank as stones.

"The same reason why you stayed in your room all day?"

"I was working."

"When did you get back here?"

"I went first to San Francisco. I had business up there."

He took out a notebook.

"Where did you stay?"

I told him.

"I left on Thursday night and arrived back here at midnight,"
I said. "If you want confirmation of that you can check with the
ticket collector at the station who knows me well, and with the taxi
driver, Sol White, who drove me home."

Keary wrote in his notebook, then with a grunt he heaved himself
to his feet.

"Well, okay, Mr. Halliday. This will take care of it. I don't
reckon to bother you again. I was just tying up the loose ends. After
all, we know who killed her."

I stared at him.

"You know? Who killed her?"

"Jinx Mandon. Who else do you imagine killed her?"

"It could have been anyone, couldn't it?" I said, aware that my
voice had suddenly turned husky. "What makes you think he did it?"

"He's a criminal with a record for violence. The cleaning woman
told us these two were always quarrelling. Suddenly he blows and
we find her dead. Who else would kill her? All we have to do is to
catch him, rough him up a little and he'll spill it. Then we pop him
into the gas chamber, There's nothing to it."

"To me that doesn't prove he did it," I said.

"Doesn't it?" He lifted his heavy shoulders in an indifferent
shrug. "I like him for the job, and the jury will like him too."

Nodding to me, he opened the door and went out.

II

So Rima was dead!

But I felt no relief, only remorse. I had been responsible for her
death.

With her had died my past. I had now only to sit tight and do
nothing to be free of the threat of arrest.

But suppose they caught Vasari! Suppose they sent him to the gas
chamber for a murder I knew he hadn't committed?

I knew he hadn't murdered Rima. Wilbur had done it and I could prove he had done it, but to prove it I would have to tell the police the whole story, and then I would be put on trial for the Studio guard's murder.

Was this nightmare never going to end?

I thought: You have saved yourself; to hell with Vasari! He is a criminal with a record for violence. Why should you sacrifice yourself for him?

During the next six days the pressure of work and the rushed visits to the sanatorium to see Sarita so occupied my mind during the day that I was free of the tormenting thought that I had been responsible for Rima's death. But at night, when I was alone in the dark, the picture of her lying in the pool of blood, her body covered with vicious stab wounds, haunted me.

I watched the newspapers for any news of the murder. It had started off as headline news, but quickly dwindled to a small paragraph on the back page. The papers said the police were still looking for Mandon who, they hoped, would help them in their inquiries, but, so far, there was no trace of him.

As one day followed the next, I began to be more hopeful. Maybe Vasari had got out of the country. Maybe he would never be found.

I wondered what had happened to Wilbur. Several times I was tempted to call the Anderson Hotel in San Francisco to find out if he was back there, but I decided against it.

Sarita was still making progress. I went to the sanatorium every evening, and spent an hour talking to her, telling her about the bridge, what I had been doing, how I was managing without her.

Zimmerman said he felt confident now that she would be able to walk again, but it would take time. He thought in another two weeks she could go home. She would have to have a nurse to take care of her, but he thought she would make quicker progress in her home than remaining at the sanatorium.

There was now no further news of the murder in any of the papers. I told myself that it was going to be all right. Vasari must have got out of the country. They were never going to find him.

Then, one evening on my return from the sanatorium, as I stopped my car outside my apartment block, I saw a large man leaning against the wall as if waiting for someone.

I recognised the big, heavy figure immediately: it was Detective Sergeant Keary.

I felt a rush of blood up my spine as I stared at him through the window of the car. My mouth turned dry and I had to fight off a panic-stricken urge to start the car again and drive away.

137

It was now three weeks since I had seen him and I had hoped I had seen the last of him. Yet here he was, obviously waiting for me.

I took my time getting out of the car, and by the time I reached him I had my panic under control.

"Hello, sergeant," I said. "What are you doing here?"

"Waiting for you' he said curtly. "They told me you had gone to the hospital so I came around here."

"What do you want?" I found it impossible to keep my voice steady. "What is it now?"

"We'll talk about that inside, Mr. Halliday. You lead the way, will you?"

I went up the steps, across the lobby to my apartment.

Keary followed me.

"They tell me your wife has been pretty ill.' he said, as we entered the lounge. "She better now?"

I threw my hat and raincoat on a chair and went over to the fireplace and faced him.

"Yes, she is a lot better now, thank you," I said.

He selected the largest and most comfortable chair in the room and sat down. He took off his hat and laid it on the floor by his side. Then he started on the routine of unwrapping a piece of chewing gum.

"When I last saw you, Mr. Halliday," he said, his eyes intent on the chewing gum, "you told me you didn't know nor had you ever heard of Rima Marshall."

I thrust my clenched fists into my trousers pockets. My heart was thudding so violently I was scared he would hear it.

"That's right," I said.

He looked up then, and the small green eyes stared fixedly at me.

"I have reason to believe you were lying, Mr. Halliday, and that you did know the dead woman."

"What makes you think that?" I said.

"A photograph of the dead woman has been published in the papers. A man named Joe Masini, who owns the Calloway Hotel, has volunteered information. He is a friend of the Marshall woman. He says she had a meeting at his hotel with a man with a scar on his face and drooping right eyelid. She appeared to be frightened of this man, and she asked Masini to stop this man from following her when she left the hotel. The description of this man with the scar fits you, Mr. Halliday.

I didn't say anything.

Keary chewed slowly as he continued to stare at me.

"The Marshall woman has a banking account in Santa Barba," he

138

went on. "I checked it yesterday. Two sums of ten thousand dollars were paid into her account over the period of the past six weeks. Both these amounts were drawn on your account. Do you still say you didn't know this woman?"

I moved to a chair and sat down.

"Yes, I knew her."

"Why did you give her all this money?"

"That's rather obvious, isn't it? She was blackmailing me."

He shifted in his chair.

"Yeah, that's the way I figured it Why was she blackmailing you?"

"Does that matter? I didn't kill her, and you know it."

He chewed some more while he stared at me.

"You didn't kill her, although blackmail is a good motive for murder. You didn't kill her because you couldn't have killed her. You were right here when she died. I've checked that."

I waited, my breathing hard and fast.

"If you had told the truth in the first place, Mr. Halliday, You would have saved me a lot of work. You went to Santa Barba to meet this woman?"

"I went there to find her," I said. "I was going to ask her for time to pay the next blackmail instalment. I needed the money to pay for my wife's operation, but I didn't find her. I was pressed for time. I tried twice, but each time I failed to find her."

"What happened? Did you pay her?"

"No. She died before I had to pay her."

"Pretty convenient for you, wasn't it?"

"Yes."

"Why was she blackmailing you?"

That was something I wasn't going to tell him.

"The usual thing-I ran into her, had an association with her, she found out I was married, and threatened to tell my wife."

He rubbed the end of his fleshy nose, his expression bored.

"She was asking big money for that kind of blackmail, wasn't she?"

"She had me over a barrel. My wife was desperately ill. Any kind of a shock would have been fatal to her."

He hunched his massive shoulders as he said, "You realise, Mr. Halliday, it is a serious business to tell lies in a murder investigation?"

"Yes, I realise that."

"If you had admitted in the first place knowing this woman you would have saved me a hell of a lot of work."

139

"An association with a woman like that is something no one likes to admit to," I said.

"Yeah." He scratched the side of his fleshy face. "Well, okay, I guess this takes care of it. You don't have to worry any more about it. I'm not making a report. I'm just tying up the loose ends."

It was my turn to stare at him.

"You're not making a report?"

"I'm in charge of this investigation." He stretched out his long, thick legs. "I don't see any reason to get a guy into trouble because he takes a roll in the hay." His fleshy face suddenly relaxed into a grin: it wasn't a pleasant grin: it was more a leer than a grin. "I wanted to be sure you had nothing to do with her death and I'm sure of it." The leering grin widened. "You can count yourself lucky I'm retiring at the end of the month. I might not be so soft with you if I wasn't going out to grass. You might not think it to look at me but I'm nudging sixty and that's the time for a man to retire."

There was something about him I disliked. I couldn't put my finger on it, but I was suspicious of him. He suddenly no longer seemed a cop. He was a man who had done his work, and was now in a vacuum. I hated having him in my apartment.

"No, I wouldn't believe it, sergeant," I said. "Well, thanks."

"We use our discretion in blackmail cases." He grinned again. "We get plenty of that. Guys making goddam fools of themselves with some whore and then getting into a mess. You're lucky, Mr. Halliday, that Mandon stopped her mouth."

"She was a blackmailer," I said. "She could have been killed by any of her victims. Have you thought of that?"

"Mandon killed her. There's no question about that."

I very nearly told him about Wilbur, but I didn't. If I brought Wilbur into it, the story of the Studio robbery and the shooting of the guard would have to come out, and then I would be fixed.

"Well, thanks again, sergeant."

He heaved himself to his feet.

"That's okay, Mr. Halliday. You're not going to hear any more about this." He looked at me, a half leer, half grin on his face. "Of course, if you're all that grateful, maybe a small donation to the police sports fund might be in order: just a thought, Mr. Halliday, not even a suggestion."

It was my turn to stare at him.

"Why, yes, of course." I took out my wallet. "What would you suggest, sergeant?"

"Anything you like." The small eyes were suddenly greedy. "Suppose we say a hundred bucks?"

140

I gave him twenty five-dollar bills.

"I'll send you a receipt. The boys will certainly appreciate this."
The bills disappeared into his pocket. "Thanks, Mr. Halliday."

I wasn't that much of a mug.

"You don't have to send me a receipt. I would rather not have it."

The leering grin widened.

"Just as you like, Mr. Halliday. Well, anyway-thanks."

I watched him go.

I had been lucky, almost too lucky.

But what if they caught Vasari?

CHAPTER NINE

I

THE following afternoon, while I was working in the office, Clara came in to tell me Mr. Terrell was asking to see me.

For a moment or so I couldn't place the name, then I remembered he was the owner of the cottage on Simeon's Hill that Sarita had been so anxious to have, and that seemed a long way into the past.

I pushed aside the papers on my desk and told Clara to bring him in.

Terrell was a man around sixty three or four, heavily built and jovial: he looked like a benign, well red bishop.

"Mr. Halliday," he said, as he shook hands, "I heard Sarita is coming out of hospital next week. I have a proposition that may interest you."

I asked him to sit down.

"What's the proposition, Mr. Terrell?"

"The sale of my place has fallen through. The buyer has found something nearer his work. My wife and I are off to Miami at the end of the week. I know Sarita had set her heart on our place. I'm going to suggest you take it over just as it stands at a nominal rent: say twenty dollars a week until she gets better. Then if you like it, maybe you would reconsider buying it, but that's up to you. My wife and I are very fond of Sarita, and we think it would give her a lot of pleasure to come straight from hospital to our place. How about it?"

For a moment I couldn't believe my ears, then I started to my feet and grabbed his hand.

"It's a wonderful idea! I can't thank you enough! Of course, I'll accept! But here's what I would like to do. I'll give you a cheque right now for ten thousand dollars and as soon as I get these operations and doctor's bills out of my hair, I'll pay you the balance. It's a sale!"

And that's how it was arranged.

I didn't tell Sarita. I wanted to see her expression when the ambulance pulled up outside Terrell's cottage.

Helen Mathison helped me to take our personal things to the cottage. We had six clear days to prepare the place before Sarita left the sanatorium. I was working long hours at the office, spending my nights at the cottage, but in spite of being so preoccupied, every now and then, I would think of Vasari and wonder. Every morning I scanned the newspapers to make sure he hadn't been found, but there seemed to be no interest now in the murder. During the past days there had been no mention of it in the papers.

Finally the day came when Sarita was to leave the sanatorium. I took the afternoon off. Helen drove me out there and left me. I was to ride back with Sarita in the ambulance.

They brought her out in a stretcher. The nurse who was going to stay with us came with her.

Sarita smiled excitedly at me as they slid the stretcher into the ambulance. The nurse and driver sat in front, and I got in with her.

"Well, this is it! " I said as the ambulance moved off, and I took her hand. "You're going to be fine from now on, my darling. You don't know how I've been looking forward to taking you home."

"I'll soon be up and around, Jeff," she said, squeezing my hand. "I'll make you happy again." She looked out of the window. "How good it is to see the streets again and the people." Then after a while, she said, "But, Jeff, where are we going? This isn't the way home. Has he lost his way?"

"This is the way home, Sarita," I said. "Our new home. Can't you guess?"

I had my reward then. The expression in her eyes as the ambulance began to climb Simeon's Hill was something to see.

All my past days of tension, fear and worry were wiped out as she said in unsteady voice, "Oh, Jeff, darling! It can't be true!"

The next few days were the happiest of my life. I had a lot of paper work to do so I didn't go to the office. I worked at home, keeping in touch with Ted Watson and Clara on the telephone.

We made up a bed in the lounge for Sarita so she could be with me. She read or knitted while I worked, and every so often I would push aside my work and we would talk.

She was gaining strength every day, and on her fourth day home, Dr. Zimmerman who had come out to see her, said she could get into a wheel chair.

"She has made tremendous progress, Mr. Halliday," he said as I walked with him to his car. "I thought once she was home she would pick up, but not as fast as this. I wouldn't be surprised if in a few months, she won't be walking."

The next day the wheel chair arrived, and the nurse and I put Sarita into it.

"Now there'll be no holding me," Sarita said. "We must celebrate. Let's ask Jack and the Mathisons to lunch. Let's have a thanksgiving lunch."

So we threw a party.

There was turkey and champagne, and after lunch, when the nurse had insisted that Sarita should go back to bed for a rest and after the Mathisons had gone, Jack and I sat outside on the terrace, overlooking the river, where in the distance we could see the men working on the bridge while we finished our cigars.

We were both feeling relaxed and good. We talked of this and that, then as Jack got lazily to his feet, he said, "So they finally caught the Santa Barba killer. I was beginning to think they would never get to him."

I felt as if a mailed fist had slammed a punch under my heart. For a moment or so I couldn't even speak, then I said, "What was that?"

He was stretching and yawning in the hot sunshine, and he said indifferently, "You know: the guy who killed the woman in the bungalow. They cornered him in a New York night club. There was a gun battle and he got hurt. They say he won't live. I picked it up on the car radio as I came out here."

Somehow I kept my face expressionless. Somehow I kept my voice steady.

"Is that a fact?" I said. It didn't sound like me speaking. "Well, that's his bad luck. I guess I'll get back to the grindstone. It's been swell having you, Jack."

"Thanks for the lunch." He put his hand on my arm. "And just for the record, Jeff: I'm terribly glad Sarita pulled through. She's a wonderful girl, and you're a damn lucky guy."

I watched him drive down the hill in his black and white Thunderbird.

143

A damn lucky guy!

I was shaking, and there was sweat on my face.

So they had finally caught Vasari!

There was a gun fight, and he got hurt. They say he won't live.

That would be lucky too--too lucky.

I had to know the details.

I told the nurse I was going down town. She said Sarita was sleeping, and she would stay around.

I drove fast to the nearest news stand. I bought a paper, but there was no news of Vasari's arrest. I might have known I would have to wait for the final night edition.

I drove over to the office. My mind was aflame with panic.

Would he die? If he didn't die he would go for trial for a murder I knew he hadn't committed. I couldn't let him go to the gas chamber.

There was work waiting for me in the office but I found it almost impossible to concentrate. I had an interview with a contractor, and my mind wandered so badly I saw he was looking at me, puzzled. I apologised.

"My wife's just out of hospital," I said. "We've been celebrating. I guess I've had too much champagne."

Later, Ted Watson came in from the bridge site. He was carrying an evening paper which he dropped on the desk. I was still working with the contractor. The sight of that paper blew my concentration sky high.

We were getting out figures, and I began to make so many mistakes, the contractor said sharply, "Look, Mr. Halliday, let's call this off. That champagne certainly must have been dynamite. Suppose I call around tomorrow?"

"Sure," I said. "I'm sorry, but I have a hell of a head. Yes, let's make it tomorrow...."

As soon as he had gone, I leaned over and grabbed the paper.

"May I borrow this, Ted?"

"Sure, Mr. Halliday, help yourself."

On the front page was a photograph of Vasari and a pretty dark girl who didn't look more than eighteen years of age. He had his arm around her and was smiling at her.

The caption under the photograph read: *Jinx Mandon marries torch singer on the day of his capture.*

The account of Vasari's capture was scrappy.

While celebrating his marriage with Pauline Terry, a night club singer, at the Hole in the Corner Club, Vasari had been recognised by a detective who happened to be in the club at the time. When the detective had approached the table where Vasari and his wife were dining, Vasari had pulled a gun. The detective had shot him before he had had a chance of firing. Dangerously wounded, Vasari had been rushed to hospital. Doctors were now fighting to save his life.

That was all, but it was enough. I couldn't do any more work. I told Weston I was going home, but I didn't go directly home. I went to a nearby bar and drank two double Scotches.

The doctors were now fighting to save his life.

The irony of it! They were trying to save his life so that he could be executed! Why couldn't they let him die?

What was I going to do?

If he lived, I would have to come forward. I had now no excuse not to. Sarita was no longer helpless. Soon she would be walking again.

Maybe he wouldn't live. There was nothing I could do now but to wait. If he died, then I would be out of this mess for good.

But if he lived ...

II

The next six days were nightmare days for me.

The press was quick to recognise the drama of the doctors' fight to save Vasari's life. There was a bulletin printed every day. One day the headline would read: *Gangster Sinking, and I would relax a little. The next day it would be Jinx Mandon lives on. Doctors hopeful.*

On the sixth day, the headlines read: *Ninety-nine to one chance operation to save gangster's life.*

The paper stated that an operation by one of New York's most eminent surgeons was to be performed on Mandon in a final effort to save his life. The surgeon, interviewed by the press, said that Mandon had only the slightest chance of survival The operation was so delicate that it would attract the attention of the medical profession throughout the world.

It was while I was reading this that I heard Sarita say, "Jeff! I've spoken to you twice. What is it?"

I put down the paper.

"Sorry, darling. I was reading. What did you say?"

I had trouble in meeting her puzzled eyes.

"Is something wrong, Jeff ?"

She was seated opposite me at the breakfast table in her wheel chair. We were alone. She looked well, and she was already restless to try to walk.

"Wrong? Why no, of course there's nothing wrong."

Her cool grey eyes searched my face.

"Are you sure, Jeff? You have been so nervy these past days. You worry me."

"I'm sorry. I was preoccupied with the bridge. There's a lot to think about." I got to my feet. "I must get down to the office. I'll be back about seven."

I had a date with Jack at the bridge site. The first girder was to be put in place.

While we were waiting, Jack said, "Is there anything on your mind, Jeff? You've been looking like hell these last few days."

"I guess I take all this a bit harder than you," I said. "I'm really worked up about this bridge."

"You don't have to be. It's working out like a charm."

"Yes. Well, I guess I'm the worrying type."

He saw the foreman was handling the girder clumsily, and with a muttered expletive, he left me and went down to where the men were working.

I would have to watch myself, I thought uneasily. The strain was beginning to show.

Two days later, it happened.

The headlines of the paper said Mandon's operation had been successful and he was now out of danger. In another week he would be flown to Santa Barba jail. As soon as he was strong enough, he would go for trial for the murder of Rima Marshall. I read the report in the evening paper that had been delivered to our home.

I felt physically sick.

This was it! Vasari had survived and now, unless I told the truth, he would stand trial and be executed.

I looked across at Sarita who was reading. The temptation to tell her the truth was strong, but my instincts warned me not to tell her.

I mustn't wait any longer. Tomorrow I must go to Santa Barba and tell Keary the whole story. He must start the hunt for Wilbur right away.

"I forgot to tell you, Sarita," I said as casually as I could. "I have to go to San Francisco tomorrow. I'll be away a couple of days. It's to do with this steel project."

She looked up, startled.

"Tomorrow? Well, all right, Jeff, but isn't it rather sudden?"

146

"We're not getting delivery fast enough," I lied. "Jack wants me to go. I've only just remembered."

When she had gone to bed, I called Jack at his pent house apartment.

"I want to talk to Stovell," I said. "I'm running up to San Francisco tomorrow. The steel isn't coming through fast enough."

"It isn't?" Jack sounded surprised. "I thought they were doing pretty well. They're sending it through as fast as I can handle it."

"I want to talk to Stovell anyway. Ted can look after the office while I'm away."

"Well, okay," I could hear the puzzled note in his voice. "Suit yourself. There's no big rush at your end now."

That night as I lay in bed, I wondered what Keary would do when he heard my story. Would he arrest me or would he first check my story? Should I tell Sarita that she might not see me again when I left the next morning? Should I tell her the truth?

What a shock it would be to her if I were arrested and didn't see her again. I knew I should tell her the truth, but I couldn't bring myself to do it.

All night, I lay in the darkness, sweating it out, and when the dawn light came through the open window, I was still undecided what to do, but finally as I was dressing I decided to see the police first.

A little after four o'clock in the afternoon, I walked into the Santa Barba police station house.

A large, well fed police sergeant sat at a desk, chewing the end of his pen. He looked at me without interest and asked me what I wanted.

"Detective Sergeant Keary please."

He took the pen out of his mouth, looked at it suspiciously and then laid it on the desk.

"Who shall I say?"

"My name is Jefferson Halliday. He knows me."

His large hand hovered over the telephone, then as if he couldn't be bothered, he shrugged and waved me to the corridor.

"Third door on the left. Help yourself."

I walked down the corridor, paused outside the third door on the left and knocked.

Keary barked, "Come on in."

I opened the door and walked in.

Keary was lolling in a desk chair, reading a newspaper. The room was small and cramped. There was just room for the desk, the desk chair and an upright chair. With me in the room, it became a squeeze.

147

He laid the newspaper down and leaned back in the chair so that it creaked. His small eyes widened at the sight of me.

"Well, well, it's Mr. Halliday," he said. "This is a surprise. Sit down. Welcome to Santa Barba."

I sat down, facing him.

"You're lucky to catch me, Mr. Halliday," Keary said, producing the inevitable pack of chewing gum. "This is my last day of work I'm glad to say. I've been thirty-five years on the force and I reckon I've earned my rest. Not that it's not going to be dull. A guy can't do much on the lousy pension they pay you. I got a small house by the sea and a wife and I guess I'll have to make do. How is the bridge getting along?"

"Yes all right," I said.

"And your wife?"

"She's doing fine."

He put the chewing gum in his mouth and began to chew.

"Well, that's good news." He leaned his fat back against the chair back and his small hard eyes examined me speculatively. "You down here for any particular reason, Mr. Halliday?"

"Yes. I've come to tell you Mandon didn't kill Rima Marshall."

The small eyes widened a trifle.

"What makes you say that, Mr. Halliday?"

"She was killed by a man who calls himself Wilbur. He is a drug addict and is out on parole."

He rubbed the end of his fleshy nose with the back of his hand. "What makes you think he killed her?"

I drew in a long, deep breath.

"I know he did. It was through her he got a twenty year sentence. When he came out on parole, he was looking for her. He was going to kill her, but he couldn't find her. I told him where she was. He went to the bungalow, found her and killed her. I had already telephoned Vasari, warning him the police were coming for him. When Wilbur arrived, Vasari had already gone."

Keary picked up a pencil and began to tap with it on the desk. His hard, fleshy face was completely expressionless.

"Very interesting," he said, "but I don't quite follow it. How did you know this guy Wilbur?"

. "It's a long story," I said. "Maybe I'd better begin at the beginning."

He stared at me.

"Well, okay. I have plenty of time. What's the story then?"

"This is a statement, sergeant, that will incriminate me," I said"It would save time if you got someone in to take it down."

He rubbed his jaw, frowning.

"You sure you want to make a statement, Mr. Halliday?"

"Yes."

"Well, okay."

He pulled open a drawer on the desk and took out a small tape recorder. He put the recorder on the desk, plugged in the microphone which he turned in my direction. He pushed down the starting button and the reels began to revolve.

"Go right ahead, Mr. Halliday: let's have this statement of yours."

I talked to the small microphone. I gave the whole story: how I had first met Rima and had saved her life when Wilbur had attacked her: how she had fingered him to a twenty year sentence. I explained about her talent for singing, about my ambition to become an agent, how I had tried to get her cured, how we had broken into the Pacific Film Studios to steal the money for her cure.

He sat there, breathing heavily, staring down at the dusty top of his desk, listening, his eyes moving from time to time to the slowly revolving reels.

He did look up and stare at me for a brief moment when I came to the shooting of the guard, then he looked down again, his jaws clamping on the gum.

I told the microphone how I had gone home, started my studies again and finally had gone into partnership with Jack Osborn. I explained about the bridge, the photograph in Life and how Rima had come to Holland City and had blackmailed me. I told about Sarita's accident and how I needed the money to save her.

"So I decided to kill this woman," I said. "When I finally found her, I couldn't bring myself to do it. I broke into the bungalow and found the gun that killed the Studio guard!' I took the gun from my pocket and put it on the desk. "This is it."

Keary leaned forward to peer at the gun, then he grunted and leaned back again.

"While I was searching for the gun, I found a box of letters.

One of the letters was from a woman named Clare Sims..."

"Yeah, I know about that. I found the letter too and I read it."

I stiffened, staring at him.

"If you found the letter, why didn't you go after Wilbur?"

"Keep going with your statement, Mr. Halliday. When you read. the letter, what did you do?"

"I went to San Francisco and I found Wilbur. I sent him a note, giving him Rima's address and I also sent him thirty dollars for the fare down here. I checked. He left San Francisco on the day she died. He came down here and killed her."

Keary reached out a thick finger and stopped the recorder. Then he opened a drawer in his desk and took out a bulky folder. He opened it and pawed through its contents. He found a sheet of paper and an envelope which he pushed over to me.

"This the note you wrote him?"

My heart skipped a beat as I recognised my printing. I looked up, staring at Keary.

"Yes. How did you get hold of it?"

"It was found at the Anderson hotel, San Francisco," Keary said. "Wilbur never got it."

I felt a sudden rush of blood to my face.

"He never got it? Of course he did! And he acted on it! What are you saying?"

"He never got it," Keary said. "This letter arrived on the morning of the 17th. Wilbur was arrested while returning to his hotel on the night of the 16th. He was arrested for carrying drugs, and he went back to complete his sentence. He is in jail right now." He picked up his pencil and began to tap on the desk with it again. "When I found the letter from Clare Sims, warning the Marshall woman that Wilbur was after her, I checked with Frisco. They told me Wilbur had been arrested. The next morning the hotel handed your letter to the police. They sent it down to us. We didn't bother further with it as Wilbur not only couldn't have killed her, but he never got the letter."

I sat there, staring at him, unable to believe him.

"Then if he didn't kill her, who did?" I said hoarsely. Keary looked bored.

"You're hard to convince, aren't you? I told you in the first place who killed her-Jinx Mandon. I told you we had enough on him to put him in the gas chamber, and that's where he's going. He was cheating with Rima Marshall. He met this singer, Pauline Terry, who was down at Santa Barba, and he fell for her. Rima found out and threatened to give him away to the police unless he gave up the girl. He was ready to go when your telephone call came through. That gave him his excuse to leave her, but she had other ideas. She went for him with a knife. There was a struggle. He went berserk and killed her. That's his story. We have the knife. We have his blood-stained clothing and we've got his confession."

I continued to stare at him, too shocked to say anything. I had delivered myself into his hands for nothing!

There was a long pause while Keary continued to tap on the desk, then he said, "Looks as if you've talked yourself into a jam, doesn't it?"

"Yes. I was certain Wilbur killed her and it was my responsibility. I couldn't let Mandon suffer."

Keary pressed down the rewind button on the tape recorder.

"Yeah? Why should you have worried about a rat like that?"

He took the tape off the machine and laid it on the desk.

"That happens to be the way I feel about a situation like this." I said quietly.

"Well, the chances are you'll beat a first degree murder rap," Keary said, "but they'll hang a fifteen year stretch on you. What's your wife think about it? Did she think it was a good idea to come down here and talk yourself into a fifteen year stretch?"

"She doesn't know."

It's going to be quite a jolt for her when she finds out, isn't it?"

I moved impatiently. His sadistic smirk angered me.

"I can't see how that concerns you."

He leaned forward and picked up the gun, examined it, then put it down again.

"What's going to happen to the bridge when you get locked up?"

"They'll find someone." I was feeling cold and numb. "There's always someone else to take over another man's job."

"Yeah." Keary shifted his bulk in his chair. "Another guy takes over my job tonight. By the time I'm half way home, all the bright boys here will have forgotten I ever existed. What's your wife going to do without you?"

"What do you care?" I said. "I did what I did and I expect to pay for it. Let's get on with it."

He closed the file that lay before him and put it back in a drawer. Then he looked at his wrist watch. He got to his feet.

"Stick around for five minutes, Mr. Halliday." He picked up the gun and the reel of tape and pushing past me, he crossed to the door and went out, closing the door after him.

I sat there waiting.

Fifteen years!

I thought of Sarita. I blamed myself now for not telling her the truth. It was the bleakest, longest half hour I have ever sat through.

The hands of the wall clock showed half past five when the door pushed open and Keary came in. He was smoking a cigar, and he was grinning.

He closed the door, moved around me to his desk chair and sat down.

"Have you been sweating it out, Mr. Halliday?" he said. "Imagining yourself behind bars, huh?"

I didn't say anything.

151

"I've been saying goodbye to the boys," Keary went on. "At five o'clock I turned in my badge. I am now officially retired. Your case is to be handed over to Detective Sergeant Karnow: the biggest sonofabitch on the force." He took the reel of tape from his pocket. "When he hears this, he'll jump for joy." The small hard eyes searched my face. "But you and me could fix it that he doesn't hear it."

I stiffened, staring at him.

"What does that mean?"

The leering grin widened.

"We could do a deal, Mr. Halliday. After all what's better than money? I could sell you this tape if you felt like buying it. You'd be off the hook then. You could go back to your wife and your bridge and you wouldn't have anything to worry about."

What's better than money?

He had used the exact words that Rima had once used. So it was going to begin all over again. I felt a sudden urge to lean across the desk and slam my fist into his leering face, but I didn't. Instead, I said, "How much?"

The grin widened.

"She was taking you for thirty thousand bucks, wasn't she? Well, I'll settle for twenty."

I stared steadily at him. "And how much after that?"

"I'll settle for twenty thousand. For that you get the gun and the tape. That's fair, isn't it?"

"Fair enough until you have spent the twenty thousand," I said, "then you'll remember me and come around with a hard luck story: they always do."

"That's your risk, pal, but you have a choice. You can always serve your sentence."

I thought for a moment, then I shrugged my shoulders.

"Okay, it's a deal."

"Now that's what I call being smart," Keary said. "I want the money in cash. When I get it you get the gun and the tape. How long will it take you to raise the money?"

"The day after tomorrow. I'll have to sell bonds. If you come to my office on Thursday morning, I'll have the money for you."

He shook his head and winked at me.

"Not at your office, pal. I'll call you on Thursday morning and I'll tell you where we'll meet."

"All right."

I got to my feet and without looking at him, I went out of the office. I had just time to catch the six o'clock train back to Holland

City. I sat staring out of the window, my mind busy. There had been no way out of Rima's proposition because she had had nothing to lose. She had been so desperate for money that she would have gone to prison with me if I hadn't paid her, but this blackmail proposition from Keary was very different. He had everything to lose. I would have to be careful, but I had confidence that I could out-smart him. One thing was certain: I wasn't going to pay him a cent. I would rather take what was coming to me than be blackmailed for life by this fat, crooked cop.

On Thursday morning, I told Clara I was expecting a call from Detective Sergeant Keary.

"I don't want you to put him through to me;' I said. "Tell him I'm out, and you don't know when I'll be back. Tell him to leave a message with you."

A little after eleven o'clock, Clara came in to tell me Keary had telephoned.

"He said he would meet you at one o'clock at the Tavener's Arms."

The Tavener's Arms was a roadhouse a few miles outside Holland City. A few minutes to one o'clock, I drove out there. Carrying a bulky briefcase with me, I went into the bar.

Keary was sitting in a corner, a double Scotch and soda on the table. There were only two other people in the bar and they sat away from Keary.

As I crossed over to him, I saw his eyes on the briefcase.

"Hello, pal," he said. "Sit down. What's your poison?"

"Nothing," I said as I sat down on the bench seat beside him. I put the briefcase between us.

"I see you've got the money."

"I haven't," I said.

The grin went off his face and his eyes suddenly became as hard as marble.

"What do you mean-you haven't?" he snarled. "Do you want to go to jail, you punk?"

"The bonds were only sold this morning," I said. "I didn't have time to pick up the money. If you'll come with me now, I'll get it. You can see the money counted, and then you can have it."

His face turned a dark purple.

"What the hell is this? Are you trying to pull a fast one?" he snarled, leaning forward to glare at me. "You try anything smart with me, and you'll be behind bars so goddam fast you won't even have time to tell your wife where you've gone."

"It's a big job to count twenty thousand dollars, sergeant," I said mildly. "I thought you'd want a professional to do it for you, but if you want to do it yourself, then I'll go to the bank now, get the money and bring it out here. I'm not trying to pull a fast one."

He glared suspiciously at me. "I'm not so goddam stupid to go to the bank with you. Get the money in twenty dollar bills. I'll count it. You get it now."

"And what do I get in return for the money?" I said.

"You get the gun and the tape. That's the deal."

"You'll give me the tape I made in your office when I confessed to being associated with the Pacific Studio guard's shooting?"

"What is this? That's what you'll get."

"How about a guarantee that you won't blackmail me further?"

I thought he was going to hit me.

"Don't use that word to me, you punk!" he snarled. "You're damn lucky to get away with this! I could have asked for thirty thousand. To get out of a fifteen year stretch, twenty thousand is cheap!"

"I'll be back in an hour," I said.

I picked up my briefcase and walked out. I got in my car and drove back to Holland City.

I returned to the office. Clara was at lunch. Ted Weston was just leaving.

"Are you coming with me, Mr. Halliday?" he asked as I came into the office. We usually lunched together.

"No. I've had mine," I said. "I have something to do, then I'm going out again. You get off."

When he had gone, I opened the briefcase and took from it a couple of empty cigar boxes and some rolled up newspaper. I threw the cigar boxes and the newspaper into the trash basket and put the briefcase away.

I lit a cigarette and was a little surprised to see how steady my hands were. I sat down.

I thought of Keary at the Tavener's Arms, waiting.

Well, all right, I thought, you gave me a bad half hour before you began to blackmail me, now it's my turn. I was pretty sure that I now had him where I wanted him. This would be like bluffing on a poker hand. Both of us had everything to lose, but I had got used to the idea of losing everything: he hadn't.

At half past one, I left the office and drove back to the Tavener's Arms.

He was still sitting there. His fleshy face was shiny with sweat and his small eyes were viciously mean. It gave me a feeling of satisfaction that he had been sweating it out as he had made me sweat it out in his tiny office.

When he saw me come in, empty handed, a red flush of rage flooded his face.

There were about a dozen people now in the bar, but none of them sitting near his table.

He watched me cross the bar, his eyes glittering and his thin mouth working.

I pulled a chair and sat down.

"Where's the money?" he said in a low, rasping voice.

"I've changed my mind," I said. "You're not getting a cent from me. Now go ahead and arrest me."

His face turned purple. His great red hands turned into fists.

"Okay, you bum! I'll fix you for this!" he snarled. "I'll damn well see you go away for fifteen years!"

"That's the same sentence as you'll get," I said, staring fixedly at him. "They treat blackmail the same way as they treat an accessory to murder."

"Yeah? Who are you kidding? It's your word against mine, and I know who they'd believe!" He looked as if he wanted to throw a punch at me. "You don't bluff me, you jerk! You either pay up or you'll go to jail!"

"I wondered why, after thirty-five years' service, you didn't get higher than a detective sergeant." I said. "Now, I know. You are just a stupid oaf without any brains. You're the last man in the world who should try to blackmail anyone. I'll tell you why. I made my statement to you before you retired. The desk sergeant will confirm I arrived at your office at four fifteen. I left your office before you did. What was I doing, talking to you, unless I was making a statement? Why didn't you arrest me? Why didn't you hand my statement over to your successor before you left? What are you doing here in Holland City, talking to me?" I waved my hand to the barman. "He'll give evidence that we met here and talked. Sort that lot out, and then add this little item, and then sort if out again. You aren't the only one now with a reel of tape. Remember the briefcase I had with me? Remember I put it between us while we talked? Remember what we said? In that case was a portable recorder. I have an excellent tape of our conversation. When I left you I took the recorder and the tape to my bank and I've asked them to take care of it. When that tape is played back in court, sergeant, you'll join me in prison. You'll lose your pension and you'll get a fifteen year sentence. Where you went wrong in trying to blackmail me was that you had everything to lose. Rima Marshall hadn't a thing to lose so she got away with it, but a successful blackmailer can't afford to be vulnerable, and you are."

There was sweat on his face as he snarled, "You're lying! There wasn't a recorder in that briefcase! You don't bluff me!"

I stood up.

"You could be right, but you can't prove it," I said. "Go ahead and have me arrested and then see what happens. Throw your pension away and get yourself a fifteen year stretch. Why should I care? That's up to you. If you think I'm bluffing, call my bluff. If I'm arrested, it's my bet you'll be arrested in a day or so after I'm in a cell. My bank has my authority to hand my tape to the Los Angeles District Attorney together with a statement made by me that covers your attempt to blackmail me if I am arrested. I'm calling your bluff, you cheap crook! Now go ahead and call mine!"

I walked out of the bar and across the courtyard to my car.

The sun was shining. There wasn't a cloud in the sky.

Driving fast, I headed back to Holland City, back to Sarita and the bridge.

THE END

>>> If you've enjoyed this book and would like to discover more great vintage crime and thriller titles, as well as the most exciting crime and thriller authors writing today, visit: >>>

The Murder Room
Where Criminal Minds Meet

themurderroom.com

www.ingramcontent.com/pod-product-compliance
Ingram Content Group UK Ltd.
Pitfield, Milton Keynes, MK11 3LW, UK
UKHW040436280225
455666UK00003B/113